Frederick C. L. Wraxall, Robert Wehrhan

Memoirs of Queen Hortense

Mother of Napoleon III - Vol. 2

Frederick C. L. Wraxall, Robert Wehrhan

Memoirs of Queen Hortense
Mother of Napoleon III - Vol. 2

ISBN/EAN: 9783337349998

Printed in Europe, USA, Canada, Australia, Japan

Cover: Foto ©Andreas Hilbeck / pixelio.de

More available books at **www.hansebooks.com**

MEMOIRS

OF

QUEEN HORTENSE,

MOTHER OF NAPOLEON III.

COMPILED BY

LASCELLES WRAXALL

AND

ROBERT WEHRHAN.

IN TWO VOLUMES.

VOL. II.

LONDON:

HURST AND BLACKETT, PUBLISHERS,

SUCCESSORS TO HENRY COLBURN,

13, GREAT MARLBOROUGH STREET.

1862.

CONTENTS OF VOL. II.

CONTENTS.

MEMOIRS OF

QUEEN HORTENSE.

CHAPTER I.

MADAME DE STAEL.

The Restoration, which prostrated so many great men and again exalted many a half-forgotten name, brought back to Paris amongst others a person who had been banished from France by Napoleon, and contrived to add during her exile new lustre to her already famous name. This person was Madame de Staël, the celebrated daughter of Necker, and the well-known authoress of "Corinne" and "Delphine."

The war waged between Madame de Staël and the powerful Emperor of the French had been a long and inveterate one, and this woman, with her genius, her eloquence, and crowned with the laurel wreath of exile, had perhaps done Napoleon more injury than a whole army of enemies.

Both parties hated each other cordially, and yet it would have been in Napoleon's power to change this hatred instantly into love. Madame de Staël was but too willing to receive the young hero of Marengo and Arcole with enthusiasm; it was her wish to play the part of an Egeria to this new Numa Pompilius. In the heat of her admiration, and carried away by too lively an imagination, Madame de Staël in her intercourse with Napoleon had even forgotten her position as a lady. She had only remembered that she was a poetess, and thought that consequently she was fully entitled to celebrate the young hero, and hail the radiant star that rose over France with a glowing dithyramb.

Madame de Staël therefore did not wait until Bonaparte came to her, but eagerly sought to make herself acquainted with him.

She wrote the most enthusiastic letters to the returning conqueror of Italy, which pleased the

young general but little. Occupied with his
plans of campaigns and other important enterprises, Napoleon had not been able to find time
for the perusal of the poetical works of Madame
de Staël. He knew nothing of her except that
she was the daughter of Necker, which was but
an indifferent recommendation in Napoleon's eyes,
for he not only denied his admiration to the
minister's genius, but even went so far as to assert
that this man was the author of the Revolution.

With astonishment therefore did the young
general receive the enthusiastic lady's letters.
He used to show them to his friends, and say with
a shrug of the shoulders, "Can you understand
this madness?"

But Madame de Staël was not to be dis-
couraged by the cold silence of Bonaparte. Again
and again she wrote, and her letters became
more and more enthusiastic.

In one of these epistles she went so far as to
say: "It was evidently an egregious error,
an entire misunderstanding of human nature,
that the quiet and timid Josephine had bound up
her fate with that of a tempestuous temper like
his. She, Madame de Staël, and Napoleon seemed

to be born for each other, and it appeared as if nature had only gifted her with so enthusiastic a disposition in order to enable her to admire such a hero as he was."

Bonaparte tore this letter, as soon as he received it, up, and, throwing its fragments into the fire, exclaimed:

"What! this eccentric woman, this manufacturer of sentiments, dares to compare herself to Josephine? I shall not answer her letters."

He kept his word, and did not answer. But Madame de Staël did not understand this silence, or rather pretended not to understand it. Little accustomed to surrender any of her plans, Madame de Staël eagerly wished to have her own way, and resolved upon having an interview with Napoleon, in spite of his indifference.

She really did carry out her intention. She succeeded in overcoming all obstacles that rose in her way, and the interview, so ardently wished for by the one party, so long shunned by the other, took place at last. Madame de Staël was introduced into the Tuileries, and received by Napoleon and his wife. However, the personal appearance of the witty and illustrious lady was

but little calculated to disarm Bonaparte's prejudices. Madame de Staël was, as usual, dressed
in the most tasteless and fantastic manner; she forgot that Napoleon liked to see a lady simply and
tastefully attired. Madame de Staël in this conversation fired off the most brilliant rockets of her
wit, but Napoleon, instead of being fascinated by
them, felt his dislike against the poetess increase.

It was in this ill-tempered mood that he answered Madame de Staël's rather indiscreet question,—" Which woman was in his eyes the greatest?" with the sarcastic remark,—" She who
gives most children to the state."

Madame de Staël had come with a heart full
of enthusiasm and admiration; she had addressed
Napoleon as "a god descended on earth;" she
had come as a gifted poetess, and went away an
offended woman. She never forgave Bonaparte
this sarcastic answer, which reflected ridicule on
the questioner, but revenged herself by biting
bon mots directed against Napoleon and his family,
and which of course never failed to reach the
First Consul's ears.

But these weapons of wit and sarcasm,
chosen by the illustrious lady to combat the hero,

wounded deeper than iron or steel, the more so
as Madame de Staël was a perfect mistress in the
art of handling them.   Napoleon felt her superi-
ority in this respect, and his hostile feeling increased against a woman who dared to prick his
Achilles' heel with the needle of wit, and thus
wound him in the most effective manner.

An inveterate war ensued between the two
greatest geniuses of that time, a war which on
both sides was carried on with unrelenting animosity.   But the two contending parties could
not be said to be fairly matched, for Napoleon
was in power, and thus enabled to punish as a
monarch the hostility of a talented enemy.

He banished Madame de Staël from Paris, and
soon afterwards from France, and the very lady
who would have gladly celebrated in her verses
" the god descended on earth," went abroad as
a Royalist, an enemy of Napoleon, who was
anxious to use all her eloquence and genius to
promote the cause of the exiled Bourbons, and to
raise in the hearts of men an invisible, but numerous and formidable, host against her great adversary, Napoleon.   Madame de Staël's effusions
of hatred against Napoleon gained additional

strength after she had rendered her name still more famous by the composition of "Corinne" and "Delphine," and she soon was as dangerous a foe as ever England, Russia, or Austria could be.

But in the midst of the triumphs which Madame de Staël enjoyed abroad, she was soon violently attacked by home-sickness. She loved her native country passionately, and felt more strongly than ever attached to it, now that she was banished from it. She employed all the interest she could command to obtain permission to return to France, but the Emperor remained inexorable, even after having read "Delphine."

"Women," he said, "who wish to play the part of men, I dislike quite as much as effeminate men. What is the use of these aberrations of imagination? What remains of them? Nothing! All this is unsoundness of feeling, mental derangement. I dislike this woman, perhaps I dislike her only because I have no patience with ladies who throw themselves into my arms, and God knows she has tried hard to do so."

Madame de Staël's solicitations to be allowed to return met with a stern refusal, but she was quite as unwilling now to relinquish her design

as she had been when endeavouring to gain
Napoleon's affections. Again and again she tried
to attain her object, and we may well excuse her
for doing so, for it was not only the return to
France she had in view, but also the recovery of
a million of francs, owing to her by France.

Her father, Necker, had during the time of
the great famine, when misery was almost universal and money scarce, assisted his suffering
fatherland with a loan of 1,000,000 francs, that
were required for the purchase of corn, and
Louis XVI. had signed a document, in which he
bound himself to repay this "national debt."

The Revolution, however, which crushed the
throne of the unhappy king, buried all written
promises and obligations beneath the ruins of the
old time, and Necker's loan had long been forgotten by the French government.

Madame de Staël now insisted that the Emperor should keep the promise of the late king,
and demanded that the successor to the throne of
the Bourbons should pay a debt which the latter
had contracted during the time of her father.

We have mentioned already that upon the
occasion of her interview with Napoleon, Ma-

dame de Staël had addressed him as "a god who had descended on earth." It appears she still believed in the deity of the Emperor, and thought he would shower down upon her a golden rain out of his cornucopia.

As she was not permitted to return to France herself, she sent her son to plead before the Emperor on behalf of herself and her million. Well knowing, however, how difficult it would be even for her son to obtain an audience of Napoleon, she addressed herself in an eloquent letter to Queen Hortense, begging her to play the part of a mediator between her and the Emperor.

Hortense, always full of compassion for the unfortunate, felt deeply interested in the fate of the talented authoress, whom she could not refuse her admiration, and willingly undertook to be the protectress of Madame de Staël. She was the only one who, in spite of Napoleon's displeasure, again and again stood up for the rights of the poor exile, and represented her being recalled as a necessary act of justice. She even went so far in her generosity as hospitably to entertain the universally shunned son of the authoress, and introduce him into her drawing-room.

Hortense's generous and eloquent entreaties and representations achieved at last what nought else could have accomplished. She succeeded in overcoming, partially at least, the Emperor's animosity against Madame de Staël. Napoleon permitted this lady to return to France, but she was never to appear in Paris or its neighbourhood. Owing to Hortense's mediation he also granted Monsieur de Staël an audience, which for a long time had been solicited in vain.

The interview of Napoleon with the son of Madame de Staël was as interesting as it was original. The Emperor on this occasion openly manifested his ill-feeling and even hatred against Madame de Staël, as well as her father, whilst at the same time he listened generously to the defence made by the son and grandson.

Young de Staël represented to the Emperor the impatience of his mother to return to her native country, and told him how lonely and wretched she felt in her exile.

"Oh, nonsense," the Emperor replied, " your mother is an eccentric woman. I will not say that she is bad. She possesses talent, much talent, in fact, far too much, but hers is an

offensive, a revolutionary talent. She grew up
in the chaos of a falling monarchy and a revolution, and bears the stamp of both on her mind.
All this may become dangerous. Possessed, as
she undoubtedly is, of considerable genius, she
may be successful in making proselytes, and I
must therefore watch her. I know she does not
like me; and it is for the sake of those whom she
would attack, that I do not allow her to come to
Paris. Suppose I were to do so? Before six
months had passed she would have reduced me
to the painful necessity of sending her to Bicêtre,
or of shutting her up in the Temple. How disagreeable this would be! It would create great
sensation and prove very injurious to my popularity. Tell your mother that I have come to a
resolution which nothing can alter. As long as I
live she will not return to Paris."

It was in vain that young De Staël assured the
Emperor, in the name of his mother, that she
would carefully avoid every sort of conflict, that
once in Paris she would live quite retired; Napoleon was not to be dissuaded from his resolution.

"This is all very fine! I know what such
promises mean," was his answer; "I see at what

you aim, but I assure you it will prove a failure. She would be a pattern and standard to the whole Faubourg St Germain. She live retired? Why, they would visit her, and she would of course return those visits. She would commit a thousand follies, and cut a thousand jokes, which to her might appear innocent enough, but would annoy me. My government is no child's play, I look seriously at everything. This I wish every one to bear in mind, and you may tell it to whomsoever you like."

Monsieur de Staël had the audacity to continue arguing with the Emperor; he even went so far as to ask him, although this was done with becoming humility, for the reason of the ill-will he bore Madame de Staël. He told Napoleon that he understood the last work of Necker, to which his mother was supposed to have contributed, had a considerable share in creating his, the Emperor's, prejudices. He assured him that this supposition was without any foundation. His mother, he said, had taken no part whatever in the composition of this book, which, besides, did ample justice to the extraordinary genius of the Emperor.

"A fine justice that! He calls me the 'necessary man.' The necessary man! And yet, according to his opinion, the first thing that ought to be done with this necessary man is to make him a head shorter. Yes, I was necessary to set matters right again, to correct your grandfather's mistakes! It is he and no one else who has to answer for the fall of the monarchy and the violent death of Louis XVI."

"Sire," the young man replied, deeply moved, "you are surely ignorant of the fact of my grandfather's possessions being confiscated, because he defended the King?"

"A pretty defence this! If I poison a man and then administer to him an antidote on beholding him in the agonies of death, can I be said to have wished to save this man? Now your grandfather defended Louis XVI. exactly in this fashion. The confiscations of which you talk prove nothing at all. Was not Robespierre's fortune confiscated? Yes, I repeat it, even Robespierre, Marat, or Danton did not bring so much misery over France as Necker did. It was he who made the Revolution. I lived through the reign of terror, and was an eye-witness of the pub-

lic misery.   Well, as long as I live such times
shall not return, for that you can take my word.
There are dreamers, who know how to draw up
the most charming utopias on paper; they are
hawked about, and there are plenty of fools who
read and believe them. National prosperity is in
every one's mouth, but soon afterwards the people have no bread to eat. Of course it rises, and
this is the usual fruit of such brainless dreams.
Your grandfather is the author of those saturnalia
which drove France frantic."

After this violent and angry effusion, the Emperor cooled down to a milder tone. Approaching the young man, who stood pale and speechless
before him, and gently pulling his ear, as was
his wont to do, when after a dispute he wished to
make peace with his adversary, he said with a
gracious smile :—

"You are still very young. If you had my
age and my experience you would view matters
differently from what you do now. Your sincerity has not hurt, but pleased me; I like to see
a son defend the cause of his mother. Yours has
charged you with a difficult commission, and you
have carried it out with much spirit. I am glad

to have talked with you, for I like youth, provided it is natural and not too conceited. But
for all that I cannot hold out to you any hopes.
You will gain nothing. If your mother was in
prison I should not hesitate in granting you her
pardon; but she is simply exiled, and nothing
shall induce me to recall her."

"But, sire, is it not quite as bad to live far
from one's own country as to be in prison?"

"Oh, nonsense! These are romantic ideas.
You have learned them from your mother. She
is really to be pitied very much. With the exception of Paris she has all Europe for her
prison."

"But, sire, all her friends live in Paris!"

"With her talent to assist her, she will not
find it difficult to make new friends. I cannot
understand why she should wish so very much
to be allowed to come to Paris. Why is she so
anxious to be in the immediate reach of tyranny?
You see I do not shrink from pronouncing the
word. I really do not understand it. Why can
she not live in Berlin, Vienna, Milan, or London?
Really she ought to go to London! There she
might write pamphlets to her heart's content. In

all those places I should not think of inconveniencing her : but Paris—why, Paris is *my* residence, and there I will suffer none but people who wish me well. I wish every one would remember that. I know what would be the consequence of my allowing your mother to return to Paris. She would commit herself anew, she would seduce the members of my court, would spoil Garat as surely as she once ruined the tribunal. Of course she would at first promise everything, but she would never be able to keep herself from meddling with politics."

"Sire, I can assure you solemnly that my mother would promise nothing that she did not mean to keep. She would not occupy herself with politics. Her inclinations are solely turned to her friends and literature."

"I know the meaning of that word, sir! While talking of society, morality, literature, and of what not, a person meddles with politics. If your mother were to come to Paris, I should be told every day of some new *bon mot* of hers, even if she had never made it. But I tell you I will suffer no such thing in the city where I reside. It really would be best for her to go to London.

Why do you not advise her to do so? Monsieur Necker did not possess any administrative talent at all. I have learned what that means, during these last ten years! And now once more, tell your mother that I will never allow her to come to Paris!"

"Would not your Majesty at least, if sacred duties should demand a few days' residence—"

"Sacred duties! What do you mean by that?"

"Sire, the presence of my mother will be necessary to obtain of your government the re-payment of a sacred debt."

"Nonsense about sacred! Are not all national debts sacred ones?"

"Doubtless, sire, but ours is connected with circumstances of peculiar importance."

"Peculiar importance!" the Emperor asked, rising, and seemingly tired of the long conversation. "What creditor of the state does not say the same of his debt? Besides, I am not sufficiently acquainted with your claims on my government. I have nothing to do with that, and will not occupy myself with it. If the law should decide in your favour you will have your

money, but if favour is required to obtain it, you
will expect it in vain at my hands. I should be
unfavourable to you rather than otherwise."

"Sire," Monsieur de Staël began once more,
just when the Emperor was about to leave the
room, "Sire, my brother and I should like to
settle in France, but how could we live in a
country where our mother would not be allowed
to accompany us everywhere?"

The Emperor, who had already reached the
door, stopped, and turning round, said:

"I do not care at all for your settling in
France. In fact, I should not advise you to do
so. You had better go to England, there they
like the Geneva set, the pamphleteers, and drawing-room politicians. You had really better go
to England, for in France I should rather be
against you than in your favour."

After the restoration Madame de Staël returned to her beloved and much-wished-for
France. She returned eager for new distinction
and renown, wishing, above all, to see her work
on Germany, which on a previous occasion had
been seized by the imperial police, appear in the
press. She flattered herself with the hope that

the new court would have forgotten her being the daughter of Necker; she thought every one would receive her with open arms, anxious to recognise the influence for which she strove.

How greatly she was mistaken!

At court she was received with a cold politeness, even more offensive than open hostility. The king, in speaking of her to his confidants, called her a "Chateaubriand in petticoats;" the Duchess d'Angoulême never appeared to see the celebrated writer, and never addressed a single word to her; whilst the remainder of the court openly attacked her, and tenaciously clung to old prejudices and former hatred.

Madame de Staël's efforts to obtain influence with the legitimate court remained fruitless. She was never looked upon as a powerful personage or wise counsellor, but simply as a talented writer. Her advice was laughed at, and they even went so far as to attack Necker himself.

"I am very unfortunate," Madame de Staël was heard to say to the Countess du Cayla; "Napoleon hated me because he thought I possessed wit, and here I find myself shunned or repulsed because I am endowed with common sense. Well,

I can do without them, but since my presence is disagreeable to them, I shall at least endeavour to make them pay me my money."

Thus it appears that "the sacred debt" had not been paid under the imperial régime, and Madame de Staël tried to obtain from the legitimate king what she had been unable to receive at the hands of an illegitimate emperor.

She was well aware of the great influence the Countess du Cayla exercised over the king, and she therefore hastened to seek this lady, whose acquaintance she had made some time ago under the extraordinary circumstances of a romantic love affair, and to renew the friendship.

The Countess, who was of opinion that "auld acquaintance should not be forgotten," showed herself grateful for the service Madame de Staël had once rendered her. She obtained for her friend the restoration of the "sacred debt," for by order of Louis XVIII. a million of francs were handed over to Madame de Staël. "But," says the Countess du Cayla in her *Mémoirs*, "I believe the recovery of this million cost her no less than 400,000 francs, not to mention a set of diamonds, worth about 100,000 francs."

The "I believe" of Madame du Cayla might have been transformed into a certainty, upon examining the Countess's purse and jewel-box.

Besides the 400,000 francs and the diamond set, Madame de Staël gave her friend good advice.

"Use the favour in which you stand," she said, "and lose no time in doing so, for if matters continue as they now are, I fear the restoration will soon be restored to rest."

"What do you mean?" the Countess asked, with a smile.

"I mean that, the King excepted, who perhaps does not say all he thinks, people about the court are going on as badly as ever they did. God only knows where their follies will yet lead them to. They are already beginning to mock the old soldiers and favour the young priests, and that is the surest way of precipitating France into rebellion."

The Countess du Cayla looked upon this prophecy of Madame de Staël as the offspring of un-called-for apprehension. She thought that hopes blighted and ambition disappointed had spread a cloud over the otherwise clear eyes of the poetess, which prevented her from beholding things in

their real shape. She little dreamt that the prophecy was soon to be fulfilled.

Madame de Staël meanwhile consoled herself
for the bad reception she had experienced at
court, by assembling the *bonne société* of Paris
in her drawing-room, and entertaining them with
biting *bon mots* and anecdotes, fabricated almost
entirely at the expense of the high nobility who
had so suddenly re-appeared with their inde-
structible pedigrees.

Madame de Staël also remembered the generosity Queen Hortense had shown her during the
time of exile; and not only her, but also Madame
de Récamier, her friend, who had likewise been
banished by Napoleon, not, as his enemies said,
because she was the friend of Madame de Staël,
but on account of her being one of the principal
leaders of the so-called "little Church," a reactionary society which had been formed in the
Faubourg St Germain, and was one of those opposition associations which the Emperor most
disliked.

Hortense had always taken Madames de Staël's
and de Récamier's part with great warmth. To
both she had been a generous mediator with the

Emperor, in order to recall them from their exile, and now that a sudden change had allowed these ladies to return, they both hastened to assure the Queen of their gratitude and admiration.

Mademoiselle de Cochelet has described this visit of Madame de Staël in so masterly and original a manner, that we consider ourselves justified in giving a faithful translation of her description.

Madames de Staël and de Récamier had asked permission of the Queen to visit her that they might express their gratitude. The Queen upon this invited both ladies to dine with her on the following day. She asked my advice whom she ought to invite to meet so talented and well-informed a visitor as Madame de Staël.

"I for my part," she said, "do not possess sufficient courage to keep up a conversation with her. It is difficult to be witty whilst one feels distressed, and I am afraid my indifference would communicate itself to others."

We mentioned the names of a great many persons, and I greatly enjoyed saying as each new name was pronounced: "He is too dull for Madame de Staël."

The Queen laughed, but at last the list of guests to be invited was finished. We all awaited the arrival of the two illustrious ladies in great excitement. The obligation which the Queen had laid us under, namely, "to be witty at all cost," had summoned an embarrassed and stupid expression to our faces. We looked like so many actors, who are just about to arrange themselves on the stage, whilst awaiting the drawing up of the curtain. *Bon mots* and witty remarks followed each other in the most promising manner, until the carriage was heard driving up, when our faces at once assumed a grave expression.

Madame de Récamier, who was still young and very good-looking, bearing the stamp of great *naïveté* on her features, produced the impression of being a youthful belle, watched over by a stern Duenna, so great was the contrast between her womanly and almost bashful appearance and the masculine self-consciousness of her companion. I had always heard people say, however, that Madame de Staël was a good and noble woman, and kind to those with whom she had to do. I only speak of the impression she produced on persons who saw her for the first time.

The somewhat mulatto-like expression of Madame de Staël's face, combined with the originality of her dress and her bare shoulders, either of which might have been considered handsome, if looked at separately, seemed to realise but indifferently the ideal figure conceived by our imagination of the authoress of Corinne and Delphine. I had hoped to behold in her one of those heroines she so admirably sketched, and stood speechless with disappointment. But after the first feeling of regret had once been overcome, I could not but acknowledge that her eyes at least were beautiful. But it remained a secret to me how her face could ever have allowed love to find a resting-place there; and yet she was said to have frequently inspired it.

When I afterwards communicated my astonishment to the Queen, she replied :

"Perhaps it is her being capable of much love that inspires others with some passion. Besides, a man's vanity is flattered through being distinguished by such a woman; and after all, a woman who possesses such genius as Madame de Staël can afford to dispense with beauty."

Madame de Staël entered the room with great self-possession. The Queen asked how her daughter was, who had been expected also, and who was said to be a most fascinating young lady. I believe our gentlemen would have been still more amiable under the beautiful eyes of the daughter than under those of the mother; a bad toothache, however, prevented the young lady from being present at the party.

After the customary compliments were over, the Queen proposed a drive in the park. We were soon seated on the cushions of the Queen's *char-à-banc,* which has been rendered classical by the many celebrated and exalted personages who have successively occupied it. The Emperor Napoleon alone was never seated in it, for he never visited St Leu. With the exception of him there were but few distinguished persons of the time who did not sit in it.

As the horses only walked through the park and forest of Montmorency, the conversation was continued as if we were still in the drawing-room,

and an animated and interesting exchange of
ideas continued to take place. Our guests admired the charming neighbourhood, which reminded them of Switzerland. Then Italy was
talked about. The Queen, who had been somewhat absent in mind, and certainly had reason to
be so, suddenly asked Madame de Staël:

"Then you have been in Italy?"

Madame de Staël sat mute with astonishment,
whilst the gentlemen exclaimed,

"And Corinne?—Corinne?"

"Oh, to be sure!" the Queen replied, awak-
ing from her dream.

"So your Majesty has never read Corinne?"
Monsieur de Conouville asked.

"Yes!—No!" the Queen said, in great embarrassment; "but I shall read it one day;" and,
to hide an emotion which I alone could understand, she changed the subject of conversation.

She might have told the truth, and said that
the book had appeared at the time when her oldest son died in Holland. The king, alarmed at
her great grief, followed the advice of Corvisart,
who said that Hortense must not be allowed to indulge in despair. It was resolved that I should

read Corinne to her. She was incapable of paying much attention to the reading, but yet a painful recollection of the book had remained.

Since then I had frequently asked permission to be allowed to read her the celebrated work, but always met with a refusal.

"No! no!" she would say, "not yet. This book I have identified with my grief. Its very name recalls to my memory the most dreadful period of my life. I do not yet feel sufficiently strong to renew the painful impressions."

I alone was therefore capable of guessing what caused the Queen's embarrassment when she answered the questions concerning Corinne. But the authoress of course saw nothing else in it than indifference to her masterly work, and I told the Queen on the following day that it would have been better to acquaint Madame de Staël with the reason of her embarrassment.

"Madame de Staël would not have been able to appreciate my feelings," she replied; "I feel that she has lost her good opinion of me, and must consider me very stupid. But it was not the proper time to speak of my painful impressions."

The large *char-à-banc* was generally preferred
to the handsomest carriage (although it simply
consisted of two bolstered forms placed opposite
each other), because it was more favourable to the
continuation of the conversation. But there was
no protection against bad weather, and a heavy rain
therefore sent us back to the castle dripping
wet.

There a room was prepared for the ladies to
re-arrange their *toilette*, which had been somewhat
disordered by the thunder-storm. I remained
with them for some time, retained by numerous
questions which Madame de Staël asked regarding the Queen and her sons. She had now
ceased to be witty, but washed and arranged
herself, or rested.

"There they are," I said to myself, "returned
to the natural state of life and the prosaic existence of frail humanity. These two celebrated
ladies, who are almost everywhere sought after,
and received with deference, are as wet and as
little poetic now as myself!"

I was really quite behind the scenes, but the
play was soon to recommence.

Voices were heard under the window, a

German accent was audible, and the two ladies called out, almost simultaneously,

"Why, that is Prince Augustus of Prussia!"

No one in the house had been aware of the prince's intention of visiting St Leu, the meeting was quite an accidental one. The prince came simply to call on the Queen, but it being nearly dinner-time, it was necessary to invite him to stay. This was doubtless what he wished.

Augustus of Prussia was seated on the right of the Queen, whilst Madame de Staël sat on her left. The servant of this lady had put on her napkin a small twig, which it was her custom to twist and turn in her fingers when speaking. The conversation grew very animated, and it was curious to see how Madame de Staël gesticulated and maltreated her twig. It might have been thought that it had been given her by some fairy as the talisman on which the exercise of her genius depended.

The conversation turned on Constantinople, which city several of the gentlemen present had visited. Madame de Staël was of opinion that it would be a capital joke for a clever woman to go and turn the Sultan's head, and then induce him to grant his Turks a constitution. Whilst the dessert was on the table they spoke about the liberty of the press.

Madame de Staël quite astonished me, not merely by the brilliancy of her genius, but also by the deep gravity with which she treated questions which at that time were not considered as belonging to the domain of a lady's conversation. The drawing-room talk of the time was about metaphysics, the qualities of the heart or mind, and such like matters. It was considered the monopoly of the Emperor and of diplomatists to converse on politics. His was the age of deeds, par excellence of great deeds, just as the epoch that followed was that of great and proud words, of political and literary controversies.

Madame de Staël and the Queen spoke about Hortense's poem entitled " *Fais ce que dois, advienne que pourra.*"

" During the time of my exile, which you so generously strove to shorten," Madame de Staël said, " I often used to sing this song and think of you."

As she said this her face was so radiant with

emotion that it might be called beautiful. She was no longer the woman of genius only, but also the woman of heart and feeling, and I then understood how she had been able to fascinate men so greatly.

Afterwards she conversed with the Queen for some time about the Emperor.

" Why was he so angry with me ? " she asked. " Did he not know how much I admired him ? I will go to Elba and see him ? Do you think he would receive me well ? I was made to idolize this man, and he—repulsed me ! "

" Ah ! Madame," the Queen replied, " I have heard the Emperor frequently say that he had set himself a great task, that he felt he had to fulfil a high mission, and he often could not help comparing his labours with the efforts of a man who was endeavouring to reach the summit of a high mountain, and allowed no obstacle to detain him on his weary way. ' All the worse for those who cross my path,' he used to say, ' for I have no time to occupy myself with them.' Now, Madame, you came in his way, but had he reached his summit, he would perhaps have lent you a helping hand."

"I must speak with him," Madame de Staël said, "people have misrepresented me."

"I think so myself," the Queen replied, "but you would do him injustice if you believed him capable of hating any one. He thought you were his enemy, and feared you. It did not often happen to him," she added with a smile, "now that he is unhappy he will recognise a friend in you. I am convinced he would receive you well."

Madame de Staël also occupied herself much with the little princes, but she was not very successful in her endeavours to make friends with them. Perhaps it was to test their faculties that she asked them a great many trying questions.

"Do you love your uncle?"

"Very much, Madame!"

"Shall you be as fond of war as he was?"

"I should, if war did not cause so much misery."

"Is it true that your uncle made you repeat frequently a fable which begins, 'The stronger is always in the right?'"

"Madame, we had to repeat fables very often, but one not more frequently than others."

Prince Napoleon, who was gifted with great powers of discrimination, and whose judgment was already highly developed at an early age, answered all these questions very sensibly, and after the cross-examination was over, said, in rather a loud voice :

" How inquisitive this lady is ! (elle est bien questionneuse.) Is this what people call *avoir d'esprit?* "

After the visitors had gone, each passed his judgment on 'them. Young Napoleon's opinion of them was least favourable, but he only dared to express it in a whisper.

I, for my own part, felt more dazzled than attracted by the two ladies. It was impossible not to admire Madame de Staël's genius, in spite of all its offensiveness and aberrations, but there was no womanly loveliness and grace, no attractive sweetness in the appearance of Madame de Staël.

CHAPTER II.

LIFE AT BADEN BADEN.

THE state of the Queen's health rendered it necessary that she should travel, and it was decided
that she would proceed, in the first instance, to
Plombières. The Queen long hesitated about
taking her children with her, from whom she felt
a reluctance to part, and the Duke de Vicenza
was consulted on this momentous question.

"As their lot is fixed in France," he said,
"you most accustom people to see them there.
Should the Queen take them away, who knows
whether they may not be prohibited returning,

and the Duchy of St Leu be entirely sequestered, which we had such difficulty in obtaining,
and whose revenues are so slowly paid. The
Queen is not being dealt with frankly, and hence
she must distrust the intentions of those opposed
to her, and give no hold to her enemies."

With reference to this advice the Queen
would sometimes say to Mademoiselle de Cochelet :

" It seems to me astonishing that people talk
about my enemies. How can I have any, I
who regarded as my friends all those who suffered and felt so happy in being useful to them !
I had no enemy in those days. Power, then, is a
better thing than I fancied it ; I do not regret it,
but I feel I was wrong in not setting more value
upon it."

Such was the way in which the Queen often
spoke, whom people had already begun to represent as feeling in despair at the loss of her power,
and setting every resource at work to regain it.

Mademoiselle de Cochelet constantly reminds
us that gentleness, impartiality, and resignation
formed the basis of the Queen's character, and
whenever she departed from her habitual calm-

ness and was indignant, it was when she had proof of injustice and falseness; then she would say eagerly:

"Ah! I did not believe the world so wicked; is it possible that it is so difficult to know the truth? I feel happy at being aloof from all that appears so contemptible in my sight. I would gladly become a hermit."

At other moments she would say:

"We must be indulgent, for the world is more light-minded than wicked. The evil it does is, doubtless, the same, but it is done without intention. It must be pardoned and be loved."

She educated her children never to have a hateful feeling. "It is the nature of things," she would say to them, "that places men in such and such a rank. You must never feel angry with those who take your place, and, if they act properly, you must possess the courage to allow it and do them justice, under whatever circumstances you may be brought into contact with them."

The government of the Restoration behaved shabbily to the Queen, for it had seized on her income and the arrears due from the treasury. This was so unjust that it was supposed to be a temporary measure, but in the meanwhile, as the Queen must live, she thought about selling the precious articles she possessed. The Viceroy and the Queen also wished to sell at once the pictures at Malmaison, in order to pay their mother's debts. Eugène raised some money on his mother's jewellery, and this eventually gave rise to the calumny that Hortense was actively engaged in bringing about the return of the Emperor from Elba.

When the moment arrived for the Queen to leave St Leu, her agony at the idea of separating from her children grew greater. To give herself courage she repeated all the reasons that had decided her, and said to her companion:

" I leave my children in France, in their country, the country saw that their birth, which received them with such acclamations, and I know not why I tremble at parting from them. It is not reasonable, for what can happen to them here? the first peasant would be their defender, if any misfortune menaced them. Had they been obliged to quit France I should have had greater reason for alarm. I should have taken them among peoples too wearied of our victories, and who can feel no sympathy, either for the French name or for those who bear it."

Mademoiselle de Cochelet shared her ideas, and reassured her as well as she could in the natural anxiety she felt at parting from beings who were at once so dear and so interesting.

The Queen left her boys with Madame de Boubers, who took care of them like a second mother, under the guardianship of Monsieur Devaux, who was not to leave them for a single moment, and the surveillance of the worthy Abbé Bertrand, who gave the elder boy lessons in Latin, and taught the younger to read. These two gentlemen were the only members of her household the Queen had retained, and though through their age not very vigorous defenders, their prudence, zeal, and devotion were a guarantee that they would defend the precious treasures confided to them from all accidents.

The Queen set out, only accompanied by Mademoiselle de Cochelet, and after staying for a time at Plombières, she received a letter from her brother Eugène, begging her to come to Baden Baden, which little watering-place was at the moment crowded with crowned heads. The most marked character was Eugène's father-in-law, the excellent King of Bavaria, who had a mania for buying pretty bonnets for his relatives. Another noble character was the Grand-duchess Stephanie of Baden, who, since the fall of the Emperor, was treated with great contumely by her husband's relatives. It was seriously proposed at the Congress of Vienna, that the Grand-duke should disclaim his marriage, as having been driven into it by force. The most painful moment in the life of the Grand-duchess was, probably, when she received a letter from Napoleon, ordering her to return to France, as the allies were on the point of invading Baden. She said on this subject to Queen Hortense:

"I was a wife, a mother, and a sovereign, and I could not thus abandon all my duties. I dared to disobey the Emperor, by remaining in the invaded country. What various emotions I experienced! I saw all the innumerable armies pass, which were about to invade France! One day I heard that a battle gained by the Emperor had driven the allies across the Rhine, and fugitives arrived to confirm the news. A few days later I learned the surrender of Paris, and the abdication of the Emperor! So many varying sensations in so short a period were enough to kill me."

The sovereign ladies were engaged in dinners and promenades, while their husbands were thinking of political matters, and preparing to go and share the spoils of France at the Congress of Vienna, which had been put off till the month of September. The conquered party were naturally in a state of great suspense, and Hortense was before all anxious about the fate of her brother. One morning Mademoiselle de Cochelet was surprised by a visit from Madame de Krudener, her old acquaintance, whom she had not seen since 1809. She sprang up to rush into her arms, but the other checked her, and said with an inspired air:

"I have come to see your Queen, for I must save her from a danger that menaces her. I wished to come on hearing of her arrival, but God did not permit it. Persons more unhappy than she demanded my attention."

"What have you to say to her?" Mademoiselle de Cochelet asked in great alarm.

"I have come to reveal to her what God wishes that she should know. You know how

dearly I love her! I have not seen her since
1809, but I have prayed for her very frequently.
She must undergo her destiny. She is beloved
of God. The poor Queen of Prussia, that angelic
princess, and Queen Hortense, are my two celestial types of women and martyrs. God has given
me the mission to serve them. I have written for
your perusal all I ascertained for the former, and
now I know all the misfortunes that await the
latter. Since I saw her last she has lost a crown,
a brilliant position, a friend, and tender mother.
I know all this, but God loves her and wishes to
try her: she must resign herself, for she has not
yet seen the end of her sufferings."

"What do you know about all this, my dear
Madame?" Mademoiselle de Cochelet asked;
"come, let us talk as we used to do: sit down,
and do not alarm me thus about the future of a
person whom you love as much as I do."

"Yes, she will be happy with her pure, sub-
lime soul. But she must expect nothing from
man, for God alone will protect her. Before all,
she must not return to France, but go to Russia,
where the Emperor Alexander will be the refuge
of the unhappy."

"You really terrify me," said Mademoiselle de Cochelet; "what can occur to her more wretched than what she has experienced?"

"Ah! you do not know what a frightful year 1815 will be. You believe that the Congress of Vienna will terminate? undeceive yourself. The Emperor Napoleon will be greater than ever; he will leave his island; but those who take his part will be tracked, persecuted, and punished. They will not have a place to lay their heads in."

She had remained standing while thus speaking. Her short figure, her excessive thinness, her tangled light hair and her flashing eyes, had something supernatural about them, which involuntarily terrified Mademoiselle de Cochelet.

"The Queen has gone out," she said to her, "return to-morrow. I know the pleasure she will have in seeing you again; but if you wish to speak to her about her mother you will make her weep, for she cannot hear the name mentioned without bursting into tears."

"What matter her tears!" Madame de Krudener said, as she went out, "God loves those who weep, for they are the predestined. But if the Queen wish to see me, let her remain at

home, for I cannot return often. I have no
longer a will of my own, for I belong to those to
whom God sends me to relieve them; but bear
in mind what I told you; do not let her return
to France."

While saying this she went out, leaving her
auditor so stunned by all she had told her, that
she did not know whether she were awake or
asleep; she had terrified her, and she trembled
without knowing wherefore.

Mademoiselle de Cochelet had a difficulty in
recognising the author of "Valerie," who had
written her own life-history to a certain extent
while depicting gentle and tender feelings, and who
in 1809 still possessed all the charm and timidity
of a weak woman, combined with a deep sense of
religion. At the time of her visit she had the
assurance and absolute tone of a prophetess, and
she produced the greater effect on Mademoiselle
de Cochelet because the latter placed entire faith
in her words.

CHAPTER III.

MADAME DE KRUDENER.

So soon as the Queen returned, her companion hastened to tell her of the visitor and the terror that Madame de Krudener's predictions had inspired her with.

"I can recognise you in that," the Queen said. "I will receive Madame de Krudener with pleasure, for she is an excellent person whom I like very much, but to believe she is a prophetess is a different affair."

The next day Madame de Krudener waited on the Queen, and had a private interview.

After leaving her, she said to Mademoiselle de Cochelet:

"What an angel your Queen is! Heaven will reward her. But let her believe me and not return to France, but go to Russia."

When Mademoiselle de Cochelet returned to the Queen she found her eyes red.

"Well, Madame," she said to her, as she kissed her hand, "she has afflicted you."

"How could it be otherwise? she reopens all the wounds of my heart by speaking to me of all the losses I have suffered. She has so tender a mind that her words penetrate through the sympathy she feels. She tells me nothing new in speaking to me of resignation to the will of Heaven. If she did not leave that track, she might be believed without hesitation; but when she declares herself inspired and wishes to foresee the future, she destroys every feeling of confidence in me; my reason refuses to believe her, as does my religion. I only see an exalted woman in her. I suppose her to be ill; she still interests me, but she no longer produces any effect on me."

"Still, Madame, she is so perfect, so detached

from earthly things, that we may easily suppose that a soul so purified is nearer to God. Why should He not employ it to call other souls to Himself, and warn those He loves of the dangers that menace them?"

"That cannot be, any more for her than others, for, if we put faith in our own inspirations, what is there to prevent them being bad? We must reject such as not coming from God. The principle is detestable, as there is a choice to make, and only the good would be free from danger, for the wicked would take their hatreds for inspirations. Religion enlightens us better; it prescribes for us a road to follow in which we cannot go astray, as it tells us to love even our enemies, and do them all the good that depends on ourselves."

"But a great number of crimes have been committed in the name of religion."

"Certainly, because man mingles his bad passions in everything. Still, if in doing evil he deceives himself for a moment, he cannot deceive others; the good sense of each can judge at what point he departs from what religion commands. But a person who believes it possible that God inspires her has no· longer any guide but herself; and everybody is not so loving as Madame de Krudener."

Still the Queen was not prepared to deny the good qualities of the prophetess, and said in the course of the conversation from which we quote:

" Mon Dieu ! No one can respect her virtues more than I do; there is no danger in seeing and imitating them ; but I wish that your reason should discern what there is good in her, and what is dangerous. It is not that Madame de Krudener appears to me mad, when she says to me, ' Do not return to France,' for she may possibly be right. Seeing the turn things are taking, I believe I shall have a difficulty in living there tranquilly. But when she tells me that I ought to go to Russia, that the Congress will not finish, that the Emperor will return, and those who join him be ruined,—how can she know that? I answered her with moderation, that I could not go to Russia, that it was the very Emperor Alexander, whom she believes the universal saviour, who fixed my lot in France ; and I added that if the Emperor, as she assured me, returned to France, I could not forget that I was his daughter, and even if the misfortunes she predicted for those who favoured him befell me, my place was by his side, and I should not desert him."

Madame de Krudener resided at the village of Lichtenthal, in a modest house, with her daughter, a lovely girl of eighteen. The principal furniture of her room consisted of a large wooden cross, to which she knelt with those whom she desired to fortify in the Faith. Up to this time she hardly knew the Emperor of Russia, over whom she exercised so great an influence at a later date. She was even a little prejudiced against him, though it did not prevent her saying that safety was only to be found by his side. It was with difficulty that she could be induced to pay her respects to the Empress of Russia, then residing at Baden, and she merely repeated to her the warnings about the terrible year 1815.

The Queen of Holland was very anxious to introduce Madame de Krudener to her sister-in-law, and the day was appointed. Hortense led the visitor into her sister's room, and presently came running out with mad bursts of laughter, greatly to the surprise, and slightly to the scandal, of Mademoiselle de Cochelet.

But there was legitimate reason for laughter; the Princess Augusta was unacquainted with the character of Madame de Krudener, and prepared to receive her with all due formality. Judge of her surprise, then, at seeing the prophetess stand before her, raise her eyes and arms to Heaven, and speak emphatically about resignation, and misfortunes even greater than those which the Imperial family had already experienced. The Princess understood nothing of all this, but sat with widely-open mouth, while Prince Eugène firmly believed that a mad woman had been introduced. All this was too much for the Queen's gravity, and she ran out of the room for fear of laughing in their faces.

Presently, however, she returned and smuggled poor Madame de Krudener out of the room, before she perceived the effect she had produced.

We have not finished with this lady yet, however; we shall return to her at the proper season, at a period when her prophecies were fulfilled, and she once more displayed her friendship for the unhappy Queen.

CHAPTER IV.

OLD TIMES AND NEW.

THE Restoration was an accomplished fact. The armies of the allied powers had at last left France, and Louis XVIII. was now the sole master of France. He and the members of his family, together with the exiled nobles, who were returning from all parts of the world, were the representatives of old France, of France with her tyrannical government, polished manners, intriguing aristocracy, and gross immorality. Opposed to these stood young France, the generation of the Revolution and the Empire, the new nobil-

4 *

ity without any other pedigree than their own merits, who could not speak of the adventures of the "œil de bœuf" and the "petites maisons," it is true, but who could relate many a story of bloody battle-fields, and life in the hospital.

These two parties could not but be hostile to each other. There was a continual struggle going on between them at the court of Louis XVIII., but in this warfare young France, who hitherto had been accustomed to conquer, suffered daily and humiliating defeats. Old France stood victorious. It did not conquer through courage or merit, but through the traditions of the past, which, without regard to the great changes France had undergone, were once more adopted as a standard for the present.

King Louis had promised his subjects, in the treaty of the 11th of April, that their titles and dignities should not be taken from them, and the new dukes, princes, and marshals were therefore allowed to appear at court, but the part they played there was insignificant, or even humiliating. They were plainly given to understand that, although they were suffered, they were far from being welcome.

Those gentlemen who, previous to the Revolution, had enjoyed the privilege of driving with the king in his carriages, continued to possess this right, whilst the members of the Napoleonistic nobility were never admitted to a similar distinction. The ladies of the old régime had their *tabouret* and their *petite et grande entrée* at the Tuileries, but it would have been considered quite absurd had the duchesses of young France claimed the same honour.

It was the Duchess of Angoulême who set the ladies of the Faubourg St Germain the bad example of narrow-minded intolerance, and of reckless animosity against the Napoleonistic institutions. It was she, more than any one else, who subjected the representatives of the Revolution to deliberate insult. It is true that the daughter of the murdered king, who had once been a prisoner in the Temple, had sufficient reason to remember and hate the terrors of revolution, but she went too far in trying to forget and ignore that period altogether.

At one of the first dinners the newly-returned king gave in honour of his allies, the Duchess of Angoulême, who was sitting by the side of the

King of Bavaria, asked that sovereign, while pointing to the Grand-duke of Baden,

"Is not that the prince who married a princess of Napoleon's making? What a weakness to ally himself to that general!"

The Duchess forgot, or wished to ignore the fact, that the King of Bavaria, as well as the Emperor of Austria, who was sitting on her left and heard what she said, were likewise allied to that "General Bonaparte."

When she took possession of the rooms she had formerly occupied in the Tuileries, the Duchess asked her old pianoforte-tuner, Dubois, who had continued to hold this office during the time of the Empire, and was now showing his mistress the beautiful instruments of Josephine:

"And where is my piano?"

This piano had been an old spinet, and the Duchess was quite astonished not to find it again, as if thirty years had not elapsed since she had last seen it, and as if there had never been such a thing as a 10th of August, 1792, when the people demolished the Tuileries.

But it was the principle to ignore history from 1795 to 1814. The Bourbons seemed to

have altogether forgotten that between the last
levée of King Louis XVI. and the first one of
Louis XVIII. more than one night had passed.
The Duchess d'Angoulême was quite surprised
that persons whom she had known as children
had since then grown, and wished to treat every
one as she had done in 1789.

After the death of the Empress Josephine,
the Count d'Artois visited Malmaison, which,
previous to the Revolution, had hardly existed,
but had been chiefly created by Josephine.

The Empress, who took great interest in
botany, had built at Malmaison magnificent hot-
houses, where plants from almost every part of
the world were collected; for many princes and
potentates, knowing Josephine's fancy for flowers, had been anxious in the days of her greatness to show their friendship by a present of rare
plants. Even the Prince Regent of England had
found means, during the war with France, to
send the Empress several West Indian specimens,
and it was therefore but natural that the con-
servatories of Malmaison should be well-stocked,
and more perfect and interesting than any others
in Europe.

The Count d'Artois, as we have already mentioned, paid a visit to Malmaison, the far-famed residence of Josephine. When he was showed the hot-houses and their valuable contents, he exclaimed, as if recognising old friends of 1789,

"Oh, there are our flowers from Trianon!"

The exiled nobility, who had just returned to France, brought back with them the same stupid prejudices as their masters.

They had preserved their customs, manners, and claims of the anti-revolutionary time, and wished to go back to the year 1789. They had so high an opinion of their own merits that they were entirely unwilling to do justice to those of others, and yet the fact of having fled from France was all they could boast of.

For this sacrifice they now wished to be compensated.

Every one of these emigrants returning from Coblentz thought himself entitled to office under government or to a pension, and could not understand how it was that those who enjoyed them were not forthwith thrown aside. A continual succession of intrigues, calumnies, and cabals was going on, and old France generally succeeded in ousting the officers and pensioners of Imperial manufacture from their offices and stipends. All high commands in the army were given to the marquises, dukes, and counts of the old régime, who had been in Coblentz, occupied with embroidery-work, whilst France was shedding her blood on the battle-fields, and who now began to drill Napoleon's veterans according to the regulations of 1789.

At court the etiquette of former days was again introduced. This was effected with comparative ease, for the royalist gentry had preserved the manners and levity which had once distinguished them in the *œil de bœuf* and *petites maisons* of old France.

These old cavaliers despised the young generation as being too moral and pedantic, they laughed at young men who had but one mistress, and to whom the wife of a friend was too sacred a person to be approached with a dishonourable thought.

When in the company of these *nigauds* of the new school, these old gentlemen were fond of talking to each other about the " good old time," and their adventures in days gone by. In the

midst of so many innovations, which could not
all be done away with, they derived a sweet satisfaction from the remembrance of the *ancien
régime*, and when speaking of that time they
would forget their age and be once more the
young *roués* of the *œil de bœuf.*

One day the Marquis de Chimène and the
Duke de Lauraquais met each other in the ante-
chamber of Louis XVIII. They were both
heroes of that time when the boudoir was the
battle-field, and the myrtle assumed the place of
the laurel. Speaking of some event in the reign
of Louis XVI. the Duke de Lauraquais in order
to denote the time of its occurence said :

"It happened whilst I was carrying on my
liaison with your wife."

"Oh then, it was in 1776," the Marquis de
Chimène quietly replied.

Both gentlemen were far from seeing any-
thing extraordinary in such a conversation.
This *liaison* had been a very natural thing.
It would have been ridiculous on the part of the
Duke to deny it, and quite as absurd in Chimène
to feel annoyed at it.

By far the cleverest and most enlightened of

all these gentlemen of the old *régime* was King
Louis XVIII. himself.

He was not blind to the faults and mistakes
of those who surrounded him, and placed but little
confidence in his courtiers. Still he was unable
to free himself from their influence, and after
having given his people a constitution, in spite of
the opposition of the whole court and the Prince
de Condé, who used to call the constitution scorn-
fully, "Mademoiselle la Constitution de 1791,"
he retired into the interior of the Tuileries, and
allowed Blacas his Premier to occupy himself
with the details of government.

King Louis, although buried in the interior
of his palace, was undeniably the most enlightened
of all the members of the old school. He looked
many things straight in the face, to which his
councillors deliberately closed their eyes, and
felt great astonishment at finding that many of the
officers and nobles of Napoleon, who formed part
of the inventory left behind by the Emperor,
were not at all so vulgar and ridiculous as they
had been represented to him.

"They told me over there," Louis XVIII.
once said, " that Napoleon's generals were nothing

but rustics and ruffians. I think this has proved entirely untrue. That man has schooled them admirably. They are civil, and quite as sharp as the agents of the old court. We must be on our guard against them."

Whenever Louis XVIII. in an unguarded moment did justice to the merits of the new time, he inflicted a painful blow on the representatives of old France, who felt angry with him and did not always take the trouble to conceal their feelings.

Louis felt this, and in order to reconcile his old jealous courtiers he was frequently induced, quite against his inclination, to subject the " parvenus" to all sorts of humiliations.

Continual quarrels and intrigues within the very walls of the Tuileries were the necessary consequence of such proceedings, and the king was frequently much annoyed or even alarmed by them.

"I am angry with myself as well as others," he once was heard to say to one of his confidants, "an invisible and mysterious power seems to counteract me, and to take delight in undermining my popularity and authority."

" But you are king nevertheless ! "

" Doubtless I am the King," Louis replied,
" but can it also be said that I am the master ?
A king is a man who does nothing all his life but
receive embassies, grant tiresome audiences, hear
still more tiresome speeches, go once a-year in
state to Nôtre Dame, and who finally is buried
with great pomp at St Denis. But the master is
he who commands, and possesses the power to
make his orders respected. He crushes intrigues,
and is able to silence priests and old women.
Bonaparte was at once king and master. His
ministers were but his clerks, the kings, his
brothers, were nothing but lieutenants, and his
courtiers little more than servants. His ministers
and the Senate were equally servile, and the *corps
législatif* was even more humble than both senate
and church. He indeed was an extraordinary
man, and must have been a happy one, for he had
not only devoted servants and faithful friends,
but an obliging clergy into the bargain."

We have mentioned already that Louis, tired
of the continual quarrels and intrigues of his
court, retired to the interior of his palace, and
allowed Monsieur de Blacas to reign in his stead.

But this gentleman, in spite of his arrogance and egotism, understood but little of the art of governing.

The king preferred talking with his friends on literary or scientific subjects. He used to read them passages from his Mémoirs, allowed them to admire his verses, and greatly enjoyed amusing them by his witty, but not always unequivocal, anecdotes. This was far pleasanter than holding long councils with his ministers, and indulging in useless disputes. Had he not given his people a constitution, and could not his ministers reign quite as well as he!

"They wished for liberty," the king was heard to say; "well, I gave them enough of it to disarm tyranny, but not so much as to occasion lawlessness. If I had myself fixed the amount of taxation to be raised, I should have at once become unpopular. As it is, France herself imposes the taxes; my only power is to do good and to exercise mercy. All steps disapproved of by the nation must be answered for by my ministers."

Whilst his ministers were thus reigning agreeably to the constitutional principle, and did things disapproved of by the nation, the king, who was only permitted to do good, and therefore hardly knew what to do with himself, commenced occupying himself with questions of etiquette.

One of the most important of these questions was what fashions should be introduced at court; for it seemed impossible to adopt those of the Empire, and thus admit that there had really been some changes going on since the year 1789.

There was to be a counter-revolution not only in politics, but in fashions and manners also, and weeks before the first great court of the king was to take place the high functionaries occupied themselves with the question, What dress should be adopted on that occasion? They were unable to solve it, and the king therefore convoked a meeting of his confidential friends, both ladies and gentlemen, who, in all secrecy, were to decide upon the important matter.

The master of ceremonies, a certain Marquis de Brezé, told the king he considered it to be almost treasonable to wish for a continuation of the Imperial fashions during the reign of a legitimate king.

" So we shall have hair-powder and hoops again ? " the king asked.

Monsieur de Brezé remained perfectly serious when he answered, that he was thinking day and night how to escape the difficulty, but that up to the present no idea had occurred to him which might be called worthy of the Master of Ceremonies to the most Christian King.

"Sire," said the Duke de Chartres, with a smile, "I demand the introduction of breeches, and the shoes with buckles, bags, and pigtails."

"In that case," the Prince de Poix remarked, who had remained in France during the time of the *Empire,* "I shall ask for compensation if I am compelled to return to the old fashions before my present habiliments are worn out. As to the ladies, I propose that if the noble Marquis does really insist upon their being again surrounded by a wall of petticoats and wires, we may at least be excused from considering them guardians of virtue (vertugadin)."*

The Master of Ceremonies answered this joke

---

* In the time of Louis XIV. the ladies of the French court used to wear round their bodies a thick roll, called *vertugadin,* and which gave them the appearance of great stoutness. This curious article had been invented by the Marchioness de Montespan, when wishing to conceal her pregnancy.

by a heavy sigh only, and the king at length decided that every one should be left at liberty to dress himself according to the old fashion or the new one.

The Master of Ceremonies was obliged to submit to this decision, but he did it with great reluctance, and said, in quite a melancholy voice:

"Your Majesty may be pleased to smile, but I beg to remark that dress half makes the man, and that equality of dress, which must needs lead to confusion, is the mother of revolutionary principles."

"I see, Marquis," the king replied, with a laugh, "that you think, with Figaro, that there is many a man who defies a judge in ordinary dress, whilst he would tremble before his clerk in a flowing gown."

The Master of Ceremonies might have consoled himself about his defeat in the discussion concerning the dress, for he had it all his own way in most of the other points of etiquette, which now again was restored to the tyrannical sway it enjoyed prior to the Revolution.

According to this etiquette the king was never allowed to leave his bed without the assistance of his chamberlains, and did not rise until the door had been opened to all those who possessed the privilege of the *grande entrée*. It was enjoyed by the officers of the palace, the high nobility, the marshals of France, some few favourite ladies. His Majesty's *cafétier*, tailor, the bearer of his slippers, a barber with two assistants, the watchmaker, and the apothecary were also permitted to enter the king's bed-room.

In the presence of all these distinguished persons the king would be dressed. The only thing etiquette allowed the king to do in this operation was tying his own cravat. The king was also expected carefully to empty the pockets of the coat which he had worn on the previous day.

Another custom of old France was the public dinners "of the royal family," and this was likewise renewed. The Master of the Ceremonies was occupied for several weeks with preparations for the first of these dinners, and the king had to appoint special officers of the table, who had to perform the social duties of such dignitaries during the old feudal system.

At these state-dinners the famous "ship" might

also be seen again, which was never allowed to be missing on the royal table, and which stood before the plate of the king. During the Revolution of 1792, this valuable piece of plate, which was a present of the city of Paris to some early French monarch, had been lost, and the Master of Ceremonies had been obliged to order a new one from the court-jeweller.

This vessel, which was made of solid silver and thickly gilt, represented the wreck of a ship without masts, and contained the king's table napkins between two golden plates, and scented with costly perfume. According to the old etiquette, nobody was allowed (not even the members of the Royal family) to pass the " ship " without bowing, and the king's bed was the object of equal veneration.

There was another custom of old France which was revived, it was that of the king being surrounded by " favourites."

Louis XVIII. as well as his brother, the Count d'Artois, had their favourites. Amongst those of the King, the witty and handsome Countess du Cayla held the first rank. It was her duty to amuse the sovereign, and to drive away the clouds which but too often covered his brow when confined to his arm-chair by illness or dislike against exertion.

She used to entertain him with anecdotes taken from the *chronique scandaleuse* of the Imperial court, or remind him of the adventures of his youth, which the king could relate with so much wit and vivacity. Or she would examine the letters of the "black cabinet," which the general post-office sent the King out of politeness, and read the most interesting amongst them aloud.

The King used to compare this *espionnage* with the all-hearing ear of Dionysius of Syracuse, which received information of everything that was going on.

Louis XVIII. did not neglect to show himself grateful to his interesting friend. Finding that she was but little acquainted with the contents of Holy Scripture, he presented her with one of Royaumont's Illustrated Bibles. Every one of the 150 beautiful engravings of this volume was covered by a thousand franc note.

On another occasion the King gave her a copy of the constitution, and again enlivened its perusal by many a bank note.

The Countess du Cayla, in return for so much generosity, patiently submitted to being called the King's snuff-box, a name which had been given her because King Louis took a particular delight in inhaling snuff which he had previously placed on the fair Countess's white shoulder.

CHAPTER V.

THE DRAWING-ROOM OF THE DUCHESS DE ST LEU.

WHILST in the Tuileries persons were occupying themselves with restoring the etiquette and levity of Royal France—whilst Monsieur de Blacas enjoyed in short-sighted ignorance the day of his glory, and amused himself with turning back the hands on the clock of time—time progressed.

The continual struggle of the two great political parties resulted but too soon in universal discontent, whilst Napoleon, the Emperor of Elba, was secretly making his preparations for a return to France, and kept up a constant correspondence with several of his most devoted followers.

The army, he knew, had remained faithful to him. It was no secret to him that the soldiers on being reviewed by their new masters would shout "Vive le roi!" but add in a whisper, "de Rome et son petit papa."

Hortense, the new Duchess de St Leu, took little part in all this. Although still young and beautiful, she had, so to say, already done with the world. She was no longer a wife, but a mother only, and all the treasures of love and kindness that lay hidden in her heart had become the exclusive property of her children. She only lived for her sons.

In the quiet seclusion of St Leu her days were spent in study and meditation. After having painted or written during the day, or occupied herself with the education of her beloved children, she spent the evening in her drawing-room, where a few select persons would enjoy an easy and interesting conversation.

In spite of her altered position, and the comparative obscurity of her present station in life, Hortense still possessed friends who had remained faithful to her, and continued doing so even while occupying distinguished places at the new court.

With such friends the Duchess de St Leu would spend her evenings in her drawing-room, talking about the happy and glorious past; and so much did she occupy herself with bygone days, that she never perceived nor suspected how such a conversation about a great past was apt to provoke the hatred and excite the suspicion of a jealous and narrow-minded court.

The Duke of Otranto, who, through his cowardly and cunning temporizing, had succeeded in retaining the office of minister of police, which he had held under Napoleon, had his spies everywhere. He knew all that was going on in the different drawing-rooms of Paris, and of course he also knew that in the salon of the Duchess de St Leu they were compensating themselves for a dull and uneventful present by the remembrances of a great past. Now Fouché, or rather the Duke of Otranto. was the sort of man who knew how to turn everything to his own advantage.

To arouse Blacas, Louis's Premier, from his stupid carelessness and security, he expressed as-

tonishment at the minister not taking more notice
of the goings on at the castle of St Leu, where,
he said, they were openly conspiring against the
existing government, and where the Bonapartists
used to meet and concert the measures of bringing
back the Emperor from Elba. But in order to be
quite safe, in case the fickle goddess should prove
unusually capricious, the Duke of Otranto did not
neglect at the same time to hasten to St Leu and
beseech the Duchess to be on her guard. She
was surrounded, he said, by numerous spies, and
even apparently innocent things might admit of
misrepresentation.

Hortense did not heed the warning. She
considered precaution unnecessary where there
was no bad intention, and seemed unwilling to deprive herself of the only source of consolation
which was left her.

. Thus the salon of the Duchess de St Leu continued to be the meeting-place of those who
formerly had served the Emperor most faithfully.
The Dukes of Vicenza, Bassano, Friuli, Ragusa,
and Moskwa, with their wives, as well as the bold,
enthusiastic Charles de Labedoyère, and the ta-

lented diplomatist, Count Regnault de Saint Jean d'Angely, were as welcome as ever at the castle of St Leu.

The accusations and suspicions against these meetings of the Bonapartists became more and more hostile and frequent in the Tuileries, and the poor Duchess, who lived unsuspectingly and peaceably in her retirement, became the victim of envy and misrepresentation on the part of those proud ladies of the old aristocracy, who could not understand how people could admire both them and her, and felt irritated that even now, under a legitimate government, there were persons who dared to assert that the Duchess was amiable, clever, and attractive. Hortense at last became aware of the height to which misrepresentation and calumny had been carried, and for the sake of her sons and that of her friends she resolved upon giving them the lie.

"I must leave my charming St Leu," she said, "and go to Paris. There they can easily watch all my movements, and circumstances demand that I should listen to reason."

So she left her quiet and peaceful abode, and repaired with her children and court to the

capital, there again to occupy her old hotel in the
Rue de la Victoire.

But alas! so far from silencing calumny, her
coming to Paris only served to provide her enemies with new weapons.

The Bonapartists of course continued to visit
the house of the Duchess, and no entreaty or
threat could induce Hortense to shut her door
against the faithful friends of her family, who for
the sake of this very fidelity were now persecuted.

To disarm calumny, however, and to contra-
dict the rumour that Bonapartists, and such only,
had access to her drawing-room, the Duchess resolved to throw her salon open to all strangers
who were able to produce letters of recommendation, and who wished to be introduced to her.
There were many who hastened to make use of
this permission.

A select and talented circle was soon formed
around Hortense. There were the great men of
the empire, who came from old attachment, many
strangers who wished to see and admire the ex-
queen, and not a few of the nobles of legitimate
France, whom curiosity attracted, and who wished
to satisfy themselves whether it was really true

that the Duchess of St Leu was the clever, graceful, and fascinating lady she so often was represented to be.

Among all the strangers who desired to be
presented to the Queen, one of the most marked
had selected as his introducer a graceful, amiable,
and kind person, whom it would have been very
difficult to refuse.

It was the Duke of Wellington, who requested Monsieur Récamier to ask the Queen to receive him. The audience was eagerly granted,
for the Queen at that moment was unhappy about
the fate of the Emperor. According to the new
measures taken with reference to the estates of
the Bonapartists, it was not very probable that
the treaty of April 11, executed with Napoleon,
would be carried out; in fact, there was no
longer a question about it, and Government was
even stripping the family of the private property
which they ought not to have lost.

" I wish to speak about it to Lord Wellington,"
the Queen said to Mademoiselle de Cochelet;
"the English Government is said to be honour-
able, the ministers of England signed the treaty of
April 11, and Lord Wellington can demand that

the French Government should carry out its engagements with the Emperor. Since accident has left us in France, I wish to profit by it to remind the new rulers of the justice they ought to do the Emperor. He has surrendered all his private property, and all the crown-diamonds, which he paid for out of his own pocket, and which certainly belonged to him. According to the treaty he surrenders all this in consideration of an annuity of two millions of francs, and up to the present none of the engagements entered into have been fulfilled. What will become of him if he be left with no means to pay his faithful soldiers?"

When Lord Wellington waited on the Queen, she spoke to him in this sense. He replied with his English *sang froid*, and his observing eyes fixed on the Queen.

"It is an injustice which the English Government will not suffer. I will remind the French Government that the treaty of Fontainebleau is sacred, and must be carried out in its integrity."

Another person who just flitted through the Queen's salon was Count Tascher, the cousin-german of the Empress Josephine. Arriving from

Martinique at the age of fourteen, he was placed in the military school of Fontainebleau. On leaving the Academy, he was appointed sub-lieutenant, like all the rest, and specially ordered by the Emperor to join the 4th regiment of the line. "I place your cousin in the Infantry to teach him his profession," Napoleon said to Josephine; "for that arm is the soul of war."

Young Tascher joined his regiment at Freysengen in Bavaria, and went through the campaign of 1806 with it. This regiment, which had lost its flag at Austerlitz, and was not given another, having behaved well in several affairs, received a new flag from the hands of Napoleon at Berlin. Tascher, who was still on foot, and enduring in spite of his youth all the fatigues of the war, was not in a position to meet the Emperor often. Still, at the beginning of the campaign, he was summoned to the Emperor's presence, who was reviewing his regiment on the eve of an action.

"Do you feel frightened?" the Emperor asked him.

"No, sire," the young man answered.

"Do you think you will be killed?"

"No, sire!"

"And if you did think so, what would you do?"

"I would still go on, but with less heart."

"Well then, go on, nothing will happen to you."

Two days prior to the battle of Eylau, after a brilliant cavalry affair, in which an aide-de-camp of the Emperor Alexander was made prisoner, the 4th line regiment happened to be passing head-quarters, and Tascher was again summoned to the Emperor's presence. He was in the room when the captured aide-de-camp was brought in.

"Your master," the Emperor said to him, "has not had enough of war then? Your young officers of the court do not find it sufficiently long or murderous. They flatter themselves they will conquer us, but they must undeceive themselves, for the French army has different motives from yours to insure its triumph. Look at this young man, all covered with mud, who marches on foot with his regiment, he is cousin-german to the Empress Josephine. Well! he has no favour to hope except what he deserves; with such elements the French army is invincible."

At the battle of Eylau, the 4th of the line

was almost entirely destroyed. When the Emperor inspected it the next morning he appeared saddened by the sight. He seemed searching for young Tascher, whom he did not notice, and inquired with interest what had become of him. On hearing that he was slightly wounded, he sent for him, and made him *sous-officier d'ordonnance.* His state of suffering and denudation did not seem to surprise him; he merely said:

"For a Creole this is rather hard, is it not, Tascher? but you have done your duty. I am satisfied, and your worst turn has passed. What do you want now—have you any shirts?"

"No, sire, I have only the one I have been wearing for the last ten days."

"I cannot give you one," the Emperor replied, "for I have none either; but I shall send you to Warsaw, where you will have money to buy some."

He gave him an order signed by himself, without any fixed sum, and the young man only took fifty napoleons. He served through the Spanish and Russian campaigns, as aide-de-camp to Prince Eugène, and remained attached to him till his death.

It was natural that the Duchess's drawing-room in Paris afforded even more material for town-talk and slander than the parties at the Chateau of St Leu. The old princesses and duchesses, who with their yard-long pedigrees, their prejudices and antiquated pretensions, used to assemble in the Faubourg St Germain, were furious at being obliged to listen to the tale of Hortense's increasing celebrity, and sought their revenge in increased hostility.

They did not content themselves any longer with denouncing her court and in their parties, but began attacking her in the press.

Hortense was the incarnate recollection of the *Empire*, and for that reason she must be destroyed. Pamphlets and libels were published, in which the King was exhorted to be on his guard against the dangerous woman, who openly, and under the very eyes of government, was organizing a conspiracy in favour of Napoleon. He was advised to banish her, not only from Paris, but from the country altogether, and to include in this exile her children, the two " Napoleons," for to allow them to remain in France was " making the country suckle the wolves which one day would devour it."

Hortense took no notice of these calumnies and slanders. She was too much accustomed to being misunderstood and wrongly judged, to give herself the trouble to care any longer about such things. She well knew that calumnies are best combated by silent contempt. Defence never disarms them; on the contrary, it is only productive of new material for misrepresentation.

Hortense herself despised slander and backbiting utterly. She would never suffer any one to tell her things about others which could be prejudicial to them. One day, while still occupying the throne of Holland, a Dutch lady tried to poison her mind against another lady, whom she accused of belonging to the Orange party.

"Madame," the Queen interrupted her, "I am a stranger to all parties alike; I receive all persons as equally entitled to my friendship, for I like to think good of everybody. I feel unfavourably impressed with those only who try to prejudice me against others." And yet Hortense had always been the butt of calumny and misrepresentation.

"I lived with Queen Hortense," says Made-

moiselle de Cochelet in her Mémoires, " for five
and twenty years, and during that time never left
her; but I never for a moment perceived in her
the slightest feeling of ill-will against any one.
She was always good, always gentle, taking an
interest in everybody who was unfortunate, and
invariably anxious to afford assistance. And this
good and noble-hearted woman was always the
object of intense hatred and absurd calumnies,
while having no other protection than the purity
of her intentions, and the honesty and straight-
forwardness of her actions."

Hortense did not even think of contradicting
the calumnies that were spread about her. Her
mind at that time was occupied with wholly different things.

A messenger of her husband, who was then
living in Florence, had made his appearance to
demand in the name of Louis Bonaparte his two
sons. After long negotiations he declared his
willingness to be satisfied if Hortense would consent to let him have the eldest child, Napoleon
Louis.

But the affectionate mother could not, or
would not, realize the separation even from one

of her sons, and since entreaties and supplications proved ineffectual to shake the resolution of her husband, and he seemed determined not to leave the education of both his sons to her, she resolved, almost driven to despair, to have recourse to extreme measures, in order to secure to herself the possession of her children.

She firmly told the messenger of her husband, therefore, that she refused to part with her sons, and claimed at the same time the protection of the law in her endeavour to keep what was her own. She declared that the princes could not be forced to give up their rights as citizens of France by being privately compelled to go into exile.

Thus, while the Duchess de St Leu was accused of plotting in favour of Napoleon, her whole mind was taken up with the law-suit that was to decide whether her two sons would be left her. The only conspiracies in which she may probably have indulged were organized with the aid of lawyers, and directed against her own husband.

But the calumnies, accusations, and libels in the papers, nevertheless, continued. Her friends at last considered it necessary to show the Duchess one of those hostile articles, in order to obtain her permission to reply to it.

Hortense read the paper with a melancholy smile, and then gave it back.

" It is a painful thing," she said, " to find one-self slandered by one's own countrymen, but it would be useless to reply. I know how to console myself about such attacks; they affect me but little."

On the following day there appeared in the same paper which had contained the scandalous article, an open and infamous attack upon Louis Bonaparte, Hortense's husband. On this occasion she felt extremely angry. She forgot all her disputes, all her unhappiness, she forgot the law-suit even which she was carrying on against Louis Bonaparte, only to remember that he who had been so cowardly attacked, and was not present to defend himself, was the father of her children.

" I feel revolted," she said, " and wish Monsieur Despré to answer this article immediately. If paternal and motherly affection have occasioned a dispute which makes us appear to be enemies, nobody has a right to meddle with it, and it is no

discredit to either of us. I should be extremely
sorry if people were to avail themselves of this
unhappy dispute as a pretext to insult the father
of my children and the noble name he bears. It
is my duty to stand up for him, as he is absent.
I wish to see M. Despré immediately, and will
tell him how to answer the infamous article."

On the following day there appeared in the
papers an eloquent and witty article in favour of
Louis Napoleon, which shamed his accusers and
silenced them. The warmly-defended prince
probably never knew that this article owed its
existence to his wife.

CHAPTER VI.

AN INTERVIEW WITH LOUIS XVIII.

THE Queen at length made up her mind that she ought to visit Louis XVIII., because he had signed the treaty of April 11th, and the letters patent of the Duchy of St Leu. She said to her companion:

"I should do wrong not to pay him a visit of thanks, which, at this moment, has become necessary for my security. Those who invent such stories about me, do so because they fancy they will cause pleasure at court, whose obstinate enemy they suppose me to be. When it is known

that I have seen the king, they will no longer
dare to say such things, and I shall be forgotten.
Moreover, such a step will prove to the Bourbon
family that, if I wished to intrigue against them,
I would not have remained in France at their
mercy, and that, as I have decided on seeing
them, it is because I am incapable of injuring
them."

"Then you will not follow the advice of the
Emperor of Russia, Madame," said Mdlle. de
Cochelet, "who was so dissatisfied with the slight
favour shown you, and expressly bade me say to
you, 'Tell the Queen not to take any step to display her gratitude. They will not receive her
properly, for they have not the nobility to be to
her what they ought to be.' These were his very
words, as I distinctly remember."

"You know that I never blindly follow the
advice of any one : I have but one counsellor,
my conscience ; am I acting rightly or wrongly ?
When I am able to say to myself, 'I am doing
right,' all that may result from it is a matter of
indifference to me, or, at least, I have the strength
to endure the consequences. In the present
circumstances, the Emperor of Russia took an

interest in me, and arranged my remaining in
France, which I should not have done had it not
been for my sad private position, my love of my
country, and the wishes of my mother. But it
was the King of France whom the Emperor of
Russia employed to be useful to me, willingly or
unwillingly, but that does not concern me. It
was he who signed the paper permitting me to
remain in France, and it is he, therefore, whom I
ought to thank. I never wish to appear to act
unfairly to any one, and do not find the advice
of the Emperor of Russia consistent. He made
me contract obligations, and does not wish me
to offer my thanks for them. He fears that I
may not be received properly, but what do I
care? if there be the slightest impropriety I
retire; and then I shall not be in the wrong, but
those will whom I wished to thank, and who
have insulted me."

The Queen, when she had once made up her
mind, asked for a private audience of the King,
and at once obtained it. Her companion went
with her to the Tuileries and waited while the
Queen entered the King's private cabinet, which
had formerly been the Emperor's. In seeing

again all that had formerly been familiar to her, except the man whom she regarded as a father, and whose place was now occupied by her enemy, her heart beat violently. When she came out again the courtiers flocked round her.

"Well, Madame," the Duke de Grammont asked her, "are you satisfied with our King?"

"Extremely so!" the Queen answered. All the faces expanded with joy, and every one rushed forward to lead her to her carriage. So soon as they were alone, it was Mademoiselle de Cochelet's turn to ask whether she had really been pleased with the King.

"It was impossible to be more so," she answered, "he was excessively polite, even gallant towards me. At first he was greatly embarrassed, and I was obliged to be the first to speak, but when you have any thanks to offer, nothing is more easy. He produced on me the impression of being a good man."

"And yet, Madame, he has the reputation of being very false."

"I was told so, and yet I did not notice it; on the contrary, it is possible that an aged and infirm man always inspires interest when he assumes a paternal air. It was perhaps his embarrassed air that at once set me at my ease, but I felt much more so than I ever did with the Emperor Napoleon. That is not surprising, for personal grandeur imposes on everybody, and even on me, who was his daughter; I never dared speak to him save when he addressed me. While speaking to the king I fancied, however, he insinuated a desire that I should pay a visit to the Duchesse d'Angoulême. She is doubtless a respectable and interesting personage, but I have no reason for waiting upon her. I only owed an act of politeness to the sovereign recognised by the country I inhabit, and I clearly manifested to him my purpose of absolute retirement. When he spoke of the pleasure he would feel in seeing me again, I answered him that I no longer looked on myself as forming part of this world, and that the greatest isolation suited me best. He also spoke of my mother and of my brother, and praised him; but his family is said to be so full of hatred towards all connected with the Empire, that I shall certainly not attempt to come in contact with it."

It is true that what was said about this hatred

was not reassuring. In addition to more serious things, it was stated that all the tradespeople breveted by the Emperor or the princesses, and who put up their arms as a sign, had asked the same favour of the Duchesse d'Angoulême, and they were ordered to take these arms to the Tuileries, in order that she might judge what was claimed of the new sovereigns.

·The laughter and jests in the salon of the Duchesse d'Angoulême had been unending; it was doubtless considered most absurd that *parvenus* should dare to take arms, and more than that, an eagle, a lion, but, above all, an Imperial and Royal crown. It was certainly painful for those who bore the lilies, but after such a Revolution as that of 1792, it was not ridiculous. Hence, when the Queen Hortense was told of this laughter, she said:

"It is not only in bad taste, but it proves that they have not studied the new institutions of the country, and fancy they find it as they left it; but they must grow accustomed to the emancipation of France·if they wish to govern it."

This visit created an immense sensation among the courtiers. The King's head was quite turned; he only spoke of the Queen's wit, tact, and grace, so that the members of his family at length said to him:

"Arrange a divorce, and marry her, since you consider her so delightful."

Madame Campan, the Queen's former school-mistress, soon made her way to St Leu, with a budget of news she had picked up from a gentle-man of the bed-chamber. She told the Queen the following anecdotes:

"When the King was being undressed, he did nothing but praise you; he said, 'I am a good judge, and I never met a woman who combines so much grace with such distinguished manners.'

"Every one listened in silence.

"'Yes,' the Duke de Duras at length remarked, 'she is a person whom everybody is agreed to consider charming, but it is very unfortunate, and perhaps to be feared, that she is only surrounded by persons known to be your Majesty's relentless foes.'

"He was silent, the King did not say a word, but dismissed his people.

"So you must be prudent, my dear angel," Madame Campan continued, "there is nothing so dangerous as to be praised by kings, when they have no reason to support us: they create enemies by the jealousy they arouse, and rarely try to defend us against those whose animosity they have drawn on us; I know better than any one what power enemies at court possess, and I implore you to guard against them."

"Perhaps you are right, Madame," the Queen replied, "but what have I to fear from them? I neither wish to supplant them, nor to see the King. I defy them to find in my conduct a single flaw that their calumny can assail, and what is not true easily falls."

But the calumniators were intolerable; here is an instance of perverse ingenuity. The lower classes had a habit of saying to each other, "The little corporal will come to deliver us with the violets,"—that is to say, in Spring. This was distorted into a Bonapartist conspiracy on the part of Hortense, because she was passionately fond of Parma violets, very scarce in those days, and bouquets of which were daily sent her from St Leu by her gardener.

Another calumny that greatly excited the Queen was connected with the murder of a

General named Quénel. His body was found in the Seine, and it was gravely asserted that he had been assassinated by the Bonapartists, because they feared he would betray the conspiracy at the head of which the Duchess de St Leu stood. On reflection the Duchess only laughed at the calumny, and paid no further attention. We could multiply instances, but these are sufficient to show how far party-zeal carried people.

For a season the Duchess, however, was left at peace, for the court were engaged with a great event. After many a fruitless effort the court had succeeded in discovering the remains of the unfortunate royal couple, who during the time of the Revolution had paid with their lives for the crimes of their predecessors rather than their own. Following the directions of those who in the reign of terror had been eye-witnesses to the melancholy burial of the royal martyrs, the body of Louis XVI. was found in a lonely corner of the cemetery of St Roche, while that of the Queen was discovered in another part of the burial-ground.

It was the natural and justifiable wish of the King to inter these corpses in the vaults of the

Royal tomb at St Denis, and it does credit to his moderation that he resolved upon doing it quietly and without the usual show. His fine political tact told him that it would not be wise to use the remains of the unhappy couple in making a political demonstration.

But the King's court, his own relations as well as the ministers and courtiers at large, who in pompously interring the murdered king and his wife wished to punish and humiliate their political enemies rather than gratify a feeling of loyal piety, insisted upon a public and splendid funeral, and he who by his own confession was " the king but not the master," was obliged to yield to them.

Soon afterwards preparations began to be made for the solemn and pompous burial of the royal corpses, which was to take place on the 21st of January, 1815. This day was one full of melancholy reminiscences for the family of the Bourbons, for it was the anniversary of Louis XVI.'s death.

Monsieur de Chateaubriand, the talented and devoted panegyrist of the Bourbons, wrote an article for the *Journal des Debats*, in which he announced in enthusiastic words the approaching solemnity. This article created so much sensation amongst the Parisians that it had to be reprinted, and 30,000 copies of it were sold in one day.

On the 20th of January the graves of the "Royal martyrs" were opened, and all the members of the reigning family who were present on the occasion knelt down in prayer together with the thousands of spectators that had followed them.

But the King had been quite right. The solemnity, which in the eyes of one party was nothing but an act of justice, was looked upon by the other as a deliberate insult, calculated to remind them of the days of blindness and fanaticism, during which, like most others, they had allowed themselves to be carried away by the excitement of the time.

A great many of the members of the Convention who had voted for the death of the King, were still living in Paris, or even (as, for example, Fouché) at the court of Louis XVIII., and to all these the approaching solemnity appeared a deep humiliation.

"Have you heard," said Descourtis, rushing into the room of Cambacères, "do you know that the solemnity is really to take place to-morrow? Yes, to-morrow is the great day, to-morrow they will expose us to the daggers of the fanatics. Is this the amnesty which they promised us?"

"Well," said the Count de Père, who was just then with Cambacères, and belonged to the Royalist party, "I was not aware that the Constitution contains a clause prohibiting the removal of the mortal remains of the unhappy king. I think the court is not doing anything illegal."

"They want to excite the people," Descourtis replied, pale with terror, "they wish to stir up the remembrance of bygone things, and to bring a silent accusation against us. But the day may come when power will be ours again, and then we will remember it."

Cambacères had listened to this dialogue without saying a syllable. He now approached the ex-member of the Convention, and gently taking his hand, said, in a solemn voice :

"My dear friend, I wish we were allowed to appear in mourning to-morrow, and to follow the funeral car with a torch in our hands. I think we owe France and ourselves this token of repentance."

On the following day the solemn burial took place. All Paris turned out to look at it. Everybody, not even the old Republicans excepted, and the Bonapartists as well as the Royalists, hastened to witness the procession, and thus showed that they recognised the errors of the past, and repented of their sins.

The procession moved on at a slow pace amidst the peals of all the church bells, the thunder of artillery, and the sacred chants of the clergy who marched at the head.

On the canopy that overhung the funeral car could be seen a glittering crown. The grand emblem of royalty had fallen from the brow of the living, but now the car of the dead was ornamented with it.

Slowly and solemnly the procession defiled. Now they had arrived on the Boulevard that separates the two streets that bear the name of *Montmartre*.

What means the sudden and almost universal cry that testifies surprise and terror?

The crown on the top of the car had fallen down into the glistening snow of the street, after having heavily rolled over the coffins!

7 *

This happened on the 21st of January. Two months afterwards, at the same hour, and on the same day, the crown of Louis XVIII. fell from his brow, and was placed once more on that of Napoleon.

CHAPTER VII.

NAPOLEON'S RETURN FROM ELBA.

A MIGHTY message flashed through the capital of France in the first days of March, 1815, and all France, all Europe re-echoed it. "Napoleon has left Elba! Napoleon has embarked, and will soon be in France!"

The Royalists heard it with dismay; the Bonapartists with a delight which they hardly attempted to conceal.

The Queen had been paying a visit in the Faubourg St Germain, when Lord Kinnaird rode up to her, and told her that the Emperor had disembarked from Elba. She turned pale as death, and bade the coachman stop.

"What! is it possible?" the Queen said to his Lordship; "who told you that? so many absurd rumours are flying about."

"I am positive," Lord Kinnaird replied; "I have just left the Duc d'Orleans on the point of setting out after the Comte d'Artois, who started last night."

"Ah, Heavens!" the Queen exclaimed, "what misfortunes this will entail on the Emperor, on France, on ourselves!—I dare not think of it."

"Measures are well taken; all the troops are being sent over there. The Emperor has but few people with him, it is said, and it will sooner be over."

"To die thus under the fire of French arms —he! the Emperor! it is frightful," the Queen continued in great emotion. "He cannot have committed such an act of imprudence. The news must be false."

"Be assured, Madame, of what I tell you. The source whence I obtained the information is certain; people are fearfully agitated at court, and the most vigorous measures will be taken against the avowed partisans of Napoleon."

"Do you believe that my children will be in any danger?"

"I will not answer that they may not be taken as hostages; it would be a very natural step—"

"Great Heavens! in what a position have I placed them!"

The Queen's eyes filled with tears; but overcoming her emotion, she added:

"No! the French people will not allow any harm to be done them."

"The people," Lord Kinnaird said, "will become frightful, and especially towards us English, for we need not try to deceive ourselves, they have remained attached to the Emperor, and might easily get rid of us *en masse*."

"Oh no! do not believe that! they are no longer the same people as in '93. But if you entertain the slightest alarm for your wife and children, I, who have nothing to fear from the people, offer you my house as an asylum. I am going home at once to watch over the safety of my children."

The Queen arranged with Mademoiselle de Cochelet that the two boys should be sent to the country-house of an old friend till the crisis had past. At nightfall her faithful companion entered the room of the princes, and led them on foot through the garden; the nurse of the younger boy, who was constantly with him, followed them with a bundle. The valet had gone to fetch a *fiacre*, which was waiting some distance from the house.

"Where are you taking us?" Prince Napoleon asked Mademoiselle de Cochelet; "why must we hide ourselves? Is there any danger, and does mamma remain exposed to it?"

"No, my prince, it is only yourselves who may be exposed to it; she has nothing to fear."

"Very good," the young prince replied, who was so advanced for his age that Mademoiselle de Cochelet often found herself talking to him as to a grown-up person.

The Queen had requested that the boys should not be informed of their uncle's landing. Hence they allowed themselves to be led, they did not know whither or wherefore; but this act of mystery, this novelty for them of going out at night, became an object of delight for them, which they silently indulged, however, as they understood that they were being hidden, and must shun any noise.

When this great affair was satisfactorily carried out, the Queen resigned herself to her fate; but her heart was filled with sorrow and forebodings of evil.

"I greatly deplore the resolution of the Emperor," she said, "I would give everything I possess to have prevented his return to France, because I feel convinced that there is no hope of success for him. Many will declare themselves in his favour, many against him, and we shall have a deplorable civil war, amongst whose victims the Emperor may possibly be numbered himself."

Meanwhile the excitement continued to increase. Everybody was carried away by it, no one in these days would have been able to give cool and reasonable advice.

The old followers of the Emperor came *en masse* to the Duchess de St Leu, and asked her for advice, assistance, and encouragement, and accused her of indifference and ingratitude, because she did not share their sanguine expectations, but was sad whilst the others rejoiced.

The government spies, however, who surrounded the house of the Queen were not aware of the state of Hortense's feelings. They only saw the former generals and councillors of Napoleon daily enter the Duchess's hôtel, and concluded that she must be the leader of the conspiracy that was to bring the Emperor back to France.

The Queen saw the danger of her position, but what could she do to escape it?

"I find myself surrounded by nothing but doubt and confusion," she was heard to say, " and can discover no means of extricating myself from them. I must therefore arm myself with courage, and this I have already done."

The government of the King still hoped to allay the approaching tempest; hoped to be able to turn the tide of revolution, and bury those who unchained it beneath the retreating waves.

They treated the great and decisive event as a petty plot, discovered in good time, and therefore but little dangerous. Above all, they were anxious to secure the persons of the "conspir-ators," under which name were comprised all those of whom they knew that, in their hearts, they had remained faithful to the Emperor.

They were all to be imprisoned.

The police began an extensive persecution of the Imperialists. Numerous spies were constantly watching the houses of all the officers, dukes, and princes of the empire, who were supposed to be friendly to Napoleon's interests, and it was fre-quently in disguise only and through all sorts of stratagems that they escaped the hands of the *huissiers.*

The Duchess found herself at last compelled to yield to the reiterated entreaties of her friends, who earnestly besought her to look out for a place of refuge during this time of danger and uncertainty.

It was arranged that the Queen should pro-ceed to the house of her brother's old nurse, an inhabitant of Martinique, who accompanied the Empress Josephine, when she was brought to France at the age of fifteen by her father to marry the Vicomte de Beauharnois.

This good Mimi, as the Queen and Prince

Eugène always called her through old associations, had married a M. Lefebvre, who held a small appointment in a government office, while a pension which the Emperor's children paid Mimi insured these worthy people a comfortable existence.

It was decided that the Queen should go to them and await the denoumement of the terrible drama, in which she was made to play so active a part, and of which she was destined to be the principal and innocent victim. The most difficult thing was for her to leave her house without being recognised. She proposed to take the arm of M. Devreaux, but the idea was rejected, because an officer of hers might be remarked, and perhaps followed. Mlle. de Cochelet proposed her brother Adrien, who often called to take her to her mother's; but the Queen exclaimed that she did not dare go out alone with a young man : it would appear to her the most extraordinary thing in the world, and her embarrassment would be so great that the spies must notice her. What was to be done? Mlle. de Cochelet suggested that the Queen should put on her clothes and pass for her, to which the Queen consented.

Up to this time they had not thought of dress, and the Queen happened to wear on this day a very elegant morning wrapper, trimmed with elegant lace. All this had to be hidden under her companion's dust-coloured cloak. When the Queen, thus disguised, gave her arm to young de Cochelet, she began laughing so furiously that there appeared to be no end to it. She would not go out: she forgot her position, her spies, and only thought of what people would say.

"If any one recognises me alone with a young man, what will be thought of me?" she said, and in her embarrassment had recourse to laughing again.

At length the strange couple set out, and Mlle. de Cochelet anxiously awaited her brother's return. The following is his account of the walk.

"Why did you allow the Queen to go out in that lace gown, which embarrassed her all along the road? When we passed the corner of the Boulevard, some men examined us very closely, and I did not feel at all comfortable. I certainly lowered the umbrella on the side of the Queen; but as she is not so tall as you, people could not be deceived, and I trembled lest we should be followed. To heighten the embarrassment, the Queen did nothing but laugh. In vain did I say to her: 'Madame, your lace shows; ladies do not walk so elegantly dressed, and, moreover, you have satin slippers on.' Then her laughter was redoubled, and she replied, 'I had not the time to think of all that, and I cannot walk with all these cloaks, one over the other.'"

The Queen reached her destination in safety, and was obliged to hide herself in a garret on the fifth floor, with hardly any furniture in it. She was a most difficult prisoner to manage, for she required movement so much, that she insisted on going for a walk on the Boulevard, which she could see from her window.

"My legs ache," she said to her companions, "from remaining so long without walking, and if I take the air at my window, you both cry out to prevent me. Ah, how I pity poor prisoners! if I ever have any power again, I will remember this torture, and there shall not be a single prisoner in my empire."

Another remark made by the Queen is worthy of quotation. Mademoiselle de Cochelet had told her that Lord Kinnaird had conducted Madame Lallemand to the Tuileries, that she might ask the King to spare her husband, who had been arrested, but could obtain nothing. Said the Queen:

"These English dare to be men: I can understand their being envied their liberty, and that everybody should strive to obtain it. A Frenchman would never have ventured to present himself with the wife of a condemned man. It is true, though, that he would ruin himself. Hence, the institutions are bad, as they compel a man to consult his paltry interests, instead of leaving him at liberty to develope his most noble qualities."

Even the Duke of Otranto, who was suspected, and not unjustly so, of having again turned Imperialist, was to be arrested. He managed, however, to escape the hands of the police and fled. General Lavalette, who had discovered that Hortense's house was no longer watched after the spies had found out that she had made her escape, availed himself of this circumstance to use it as a hiding-place. Monsieur de Dandré, the chief of the police, who had the direction of the arrests, was greatly mortified, and was heard to say:

"I cannot find any more of these conspirators. People have talked too much of the approaching arrest of the Bonapartists, and they have thus been enabled to escape."

All of a sudden intelligence reached the excited and turbulent capital "that the Emperor had landed at Grenoble, had been received with enthusiasm by the people, and the troops, who, under the command of Charles de Labedoyère, had been sent to capture him, had one and all gone over to his side. Grenoble had opened her gates to the Emperor, everywhere he was received with open arms, and now Napoleon was no longer at the head of a little band only, but at the head of an army, whose ranks were swelled every hour. The government tried once more to deceive, by means of the press, the inhabitants of Paris, and make them believe what they knew to be untrue.

Already the cry of "Vive l'Empereur" could be heard again; Marengo, Arcole, Jena, and Austerlitz were not yet forgotten; Napoleon was still the victorious hero, who ruled destiny, and compelled it for a season to smile on him.

A general panic seized upon the Royalists. They formed the most desperate resolutions; but when they heard that Napoleon had already arrived at Lyons, where he had again been received enthusiastically, both by the population and the garrison, they began to despair.

The heads of the Royalist party assembled at the house of the Count de la Père to deliberate on the measures that were to be adopted. Persons who otherwise were hostile to each other and belonged to different political parties, but who agreed in the one point of hatred against Napoleon, were to be seen meeting in the same room to uphold the dynasty of the Bourbons and unite their efforts in the defence of their rights.

There were Madame de Staël, Benjamin Constant, Count Lainé, and Chateaubriand; there were the Duke de Némours and the Count de la Père; and around them thronged a crowd of frightened Royalists, hoping to hear from the lips of these illustrious personages words of encouragement and advice, which would restore life and confidence to the despairing party.

Benjamin Constant was the first to speak.

"Power," he said, "must be combated by power. Bonaparte is strong through the love of his soldiers, and he can only be defeated by the hatred of the citizens. His features are imposing, like the countenance of Cæsar, and we must therefore send against him a man possessed of the same advantages. General Lafayette would be the proper man for the supreme command of the French army."

Monsieur de Chateaubriand demanded that the first thing to be done by government should be the severe punishment of the short-sighted and negligent ministers, who had done nothing to prevent the catastrophe; while Lainé, with tears in his eyes, and a voice trembling with emotion, declared that everything was lost.

"There is but one last chance," he said, "to awe the usurper. We must prepare for him a spectacle of despair and grief on his return to France. When he approaches the capital, the inhabitants of Paris—men, women, and children, the national guard, and all the corporations— must leave the city and witness the entry of Napoleon in saddened silence. This despairing million, miserable only for his sake, will not fail to affect him deeply, and he will feel terrified at the idea that a whole nation should flee before a single individual."

Madame de Staël pronounced an eloquent anathema against the usurper, who was lighting the torch of a civil war that would cause unspeakable misery to bleeding France.

Every one felt moved and enthusiastic, but nothing was done to the purpose. All the fine words and speeches that flowed from the lips of these celebrated writers and statesmen were but the report of a physician who is giving up his patient as lost. The patient on this occasion was France, and the Royalists who had assembled in the house of Count de la Père began to feel that nothing could save her, and that all they could do was to go into exile and lament her fate.

Whilst the Royalists were still deliberating, or weeping and despairing, King Louis had preserved his usual composure and self-command. It must be remembered that the real state of things had been, for a long time, hidden from him. Of course he knew that Napoleon was in France, but his courtiers had told him that the people received him everywhere with dissatisfied silence, and that the army, faithful to their oath to the king, failed to obey his summons.

Thus it came that the shouts of joy which

8 *

marked the march of the Emperor, found no echo in the Tuileries. The king was labouring under a gross delusion, the natural offspring of the misrepresentations of those who surrounded him. When on the 16th of March he went to the Chamber of Deputies to address them in an encouraging speech, he was surrounded by a crowd that received him with enthusiasm ; but this crowd was not the people, but an artificial demonstration of the Royalists. The proud gentlemen and ladies of the old nobility had again condescended, as on the day of Louis's entry into Paris, to play the part which the people seemed unwilling to accept, and furnished the material for a crowd to make the king believe in the loyalty of the nation.

The king allowed himself to be deceived. Monsieur de Blacas continued telling him of new victories, whilst in reality Napoleon was inflicting defeat upon defeat, and the Royalists went so far as to assert that Lyons had closed its gates against the Emperor, and that Ney, who had been sent against him, had sworn to bring him to Paris in an iron cage—which, by the way, was an utter falsehood.

The king, therefore, was quiet and composed in the midst of the danger, when suddenly his brother, the Count d'Artois, and the Duke of Orleans, whom he thought victorious at Lyons, arrived as fugitives in the capital. They had been deserted by their soldiers and servants, and told the king that Lyons had received the Emperor with open arms. They had both been compelled to a precipitate flight.

A second and still more terrible piece of news soon followed this alarming intelligence. Ney, the last hope of the king, the only remaining support of his tottering throne, had been unable to fight against his old companion in arms, and had gone over to the Emperor. The whole army had followed his example.

Now at last the scales fell from the king's eyes. Now he had a full insight into the real state of things, and saw how cruelly he had been deceived.

"Bonaparte," he exclaimed, "fell because he would not hear the truth, and I shall fall because I am not allowed to hear it."

At this moment, and whilst the king was intreating his brothers and the other gentlemen

of his court to deceive him no longer, but to tell
him the plain truth, the door opened and in came
Blacas. He who had never ceased yet to be full
of confidence and hope, was pale and trembling.

His features betrayed to the King what the
minister had long sought to hide from his eyes.
The king had asked his court to tell him the
truth; there it stood before him in the shape of
his trembling minister.

There was a deadly silence. Every eye was
fixed upon the Count, who sobbing with emotion
thus addressed the king :

"Sire, all is lost !—The army as well as the
people are betraying your Majesty. There is
nothing left but to quit Paris."

The King staggered back. Then he cast a
searching glance round the group that stood
about him. There was no eye that dared meet
his, there was none could cheer him with a ray of
hope. There stood his courtiers, with their eyes
fixed on the ground !

The king understood the mute answer. A
deep-drawn sigh struggled from his breast.

"Well," he at last exclaimed, " the tree bears

its proper fruit. You have wished me to govern for you only, now I shall have none at all to reign over. But mark me, if I ever again should return to the throne of my fathers, I will remember the experience you have made me buy so dearly."

A few hours afterwards, when night began spreading her dark cloak over Paris, the King, accompanied by his Premier and a few servants only, left the Tuileries and fled to Holland.

Exactly 24 hours later, on the evening of the 20th of March, Napoleon entered the capital amidst the enthusiastic shouts of "Vive l'Empereur." He at once took possession of the Tuileries, and where but yesterday the lily-spangled banner of the Bourbons had been floating in the air, there was seen once more the victorious tricolor, the proud palladium of the empire.

In the Tuileries the Emperor found assembled most of his former ministers, generals, and courtiers. They all were anxious to see their old master again. There was an immense crowd at the foot of the stairs and in the corridors of the royal residence.

The Emperor was lifted from the ground and passed along over the heads of these thousands until he reached his former rooms. There was an almost deafening shouting on all sides, and the air rang with the incessant "Vive l'Empereur!"

On reaching his apartments the Emperor was received by Queen Julie, the wife of Joseph Bonaparte, and Hortense, who at last had left her hiding-place to hasten to the Tuileries and there welcome Napoleon.

The Emperor received Hortense with a cold salutation. He inquired but negligently after the health of her sons, and then added in an almost angry tone:

"You have placed my nephews in a false position by leaving them in the midst of my enemies."

Hortense turned pale, her eyes filled with tears, but the Emperor did not seem to notice it.

"You have accepted the kindnesses of my enemies," Napoleon continued, "and placed yourself under obligations to the Bourbons. But I count upon Eugène. I hope he will soon be here. I have written to him from Lyons already."

Such was the reception bestowed on Hortense by the returning Emperor. He was angry with her because she had remained in France; and the Bourbons, whilst on their road to Holland, said:

"It is all the fault of this Duchess of St Leu. Her intrigues alone have enabled Napoleon to return to France."

The first thing the Queen did after her meeting with the Emperor was to write to her brother Eugène. This letter is memorable, because it eventually gave rise to the most culpable intrigues against her.

"My dear Eugène, an enthusiasm, of which you can form no idea, brings the Emperor back to France. I have just seen him. He received me very coldly, I think he disapproves of my having stayed here. He told me that he counted on you, and had written to you from Lyons. Good Heavens! I trust we shall not have war! it will not come, I hope, from the Emperor of Russia, for he deplored it so greatly. Ah! beseech him for peace; employ your influence with him, it is a necessity for humanity. I hope I shall see you again soon. I was obliged to hide myself for twelve days, as so many stories were in currency about me. Adieu! I am dead of fatigue."

Such was the letter which was seized by the Congress of Vienna, and regarded as a proof of the Queen's active participation in the affairs of France. This letter all but sent the Viceroy to a Moravian fortress, and estranged the Emperor of Russia from the Queen.

CHAPTER VIII.

THE HUNDRED DAYS.

THE hundred days that followed the Emperor's return will ever appear in history like a myth, like an Homeric poem, in which heroes with one grip of their hand destroy worlds, and are able to call forth armies by stamping on the ground; in which a breath is sufficient to let nations wither away and others spring into existence.

These hundred days are a gigantic epic written on the page of history. All that the world possesses of greatness, splendour, and magnificence, of victory and success, and all the misery, humiliation, and shame to be found in the annals of mortality are contained in the hundred days which witnessed the restoration of the empire.

Great and promising was their beginning. All France seemed to rejoice at the Emperor's return. Everybody hastened to assure him of his unchanging fidelity, and to represent the obedience which had been paid to the Bourbons as a painful necessity.

The old splendour of the Imperial household was restored at the Tuileries. The Emperor reassembled his court, which was almost the same as formerly, with this difference only, that instead of Marie Louise, who had failed to return with her husband, Hortense presided in the drawing-room. Her two sons were called upon to take the place of the King of Rome in the demonstrations which were made to arouse the popular enthusiasm.

Napoleon tried to avert the wrath of the Emperor Alexander at his return, by sending him a document found at the Tuileries among the papers of the Duke de Blacas, which the hurried nature of his departure prevented the minister from carrying away or destroying. It was an alliance

completed between England, France, and Austria against Russia, the result of the protracted
squabbles at the Congress of Vienna.   But Alexander was not to be turned from his purpose,
even by the knowledge of this act of treachery;
all the revenge he took was to send for Metter-
nich, and show him the treaty in the presence of
Stein, the Prussian Minister.   Then he threw it
into the fire, saying, " Let us speak no more
about it, we have something better to do."

The Emperor's anger with Hortense had soon
been followed by a speedy reconciliation.   He could
not help listening to the satisfactory explanations
of the Queen, who showed him that her only motive in remaining in France had been the wish to
secure the future of her sons.   Napoleon stretched
out his hand in token of forgiveness, and begged
Hortense to ask a favour of him, by the fulfil-
ment of which he might manifest his friendly feelings towards the Queen.

Hortense, who had been so cruelly and per-
severingly slandered and calumniated by the Royalists, whom the flying Bourbons even now cursed
as the author of all their misfortune,—Hortense
begged the Emperor to allow the Duchess of

Orleans, whom the fracture of a leg had retained
in Paris, to remain in the capital, and to grant
her a pension besides. The Queen told Napoleon
that she had received a letter from the Duchess,
in which her mediation was solicited to obtain
her a pension " in her greatly distressed situation."

The Emperor granted the wish of his step-
daughter. It was owing to her mediation alone
that the Duchess of Orleans, the mother of that
Louis Philippe who afterwards became King of
France, obtained a pension of 40,000 francs a
year. A few days later an annuity of 200,000
francs was granted to another lady of the Bourbon
family. This time it was the Duchess of Bourbon
who had reason to feel obliged to Hortense.
Both ladies hastened to assure Hortense, in a most
flattering letter, of their eternal gratitude.

Hortense felt intense satisfaction at seeing her
wish granted, and was radiant with joy, and proud
as if she had gained a great victory.

" It was my sacred duty," she afterwards said,
" to help these ladies. They were helpless and
alone, as I myself had been a few days before,
and I know from experience how sad that is."

But now Hortense was no longer "helpless and lonely." She was no longer the Duchess of St Leu, but "the Queen," the centre and the sun of the Imperial court, to which everybody bowed. The haughty ladies who had altogether forgotten her during the last year, now hastened to do her homage.

"Your Majesty was unfortunately always in the country when I called to pay my respects," said one of these ladies, who wished to excuse her negligence.

The Queen only replied with a smiling, "Yes, Madame."

One of the first acts of the Emperor had been to order that the estates of all the men who had surrendered France to the enemy should be sequestered; he said:

"Those who abandoned me I pardon; but I am inflexible toward any man who betrayed his country."

The first time the Emperor saw again Marshal Soult, who was Minister of War at the period when he landed at Cannes, and who had so maltreated him in his proclamation to the army, he said to him:

" Duke of Dalmatia, are you aware that you fired canister at me ? "

" It is true, Sire; but it was a shot that could not hit you."

The Emperor appointed him Chief of the Staff, a place hitherto held by Berthier. About the latter officer the Emperor remarked :

" Why did the Prince of Neufchâtel leave France? why has he not presented himself at the Tuileries? I would have inflicted but one punishment upon him : he must have appeared for the first time before me in his grand uniform as Captain of the Gardes des Corps of Louis XVIII."

Hortense was again a great personage, and anxiously sought after. The authorities, by order of the Emperor, hastened to wait on the Imperial family, and they humbly asked Hortense to accord them an audience. There was no end to the public festivities and demonstrations.

The most significant and imposing of all these solemnities was that which on the first of June took place on the Champ-de-Mai, where the Emperor with his own hand presented his army with the new eagles, which were in future to guide them in battle instead of the lilies of the Bourbons.

It was a grand and impressive sight to behold that sea of men, which ebbed and flowed, shouting their " Vive l'Empereur," and to see the proud and triumphant veteran soldiers of the empire receiving their eagles at the hand of the man whom they idolized. These eagles, previously to their being given to the different regiments, received the blessing of the priests, who stood on a balustrade in front of the Emperor's throne. Thousands of richly attired ladies were seated behind the *fauteuil* of Napoleon, while Hortense and her two sons sat close by the Emperor.

The air was beautifully fresh and balmy, and the sun looked smilingly down upon the glittering array. The guns proclaimed with their voice of thunder the victory of Imperialism, martial music sounded, and myriads of spectators raised a triumphant shout. During this exciting scene, Hortense on her seat behind the Emperor was quietly taking a sketch of the memorable solemnity. She had a presentiment in her breast that told her it would be the last of Imperial France.

Hortense was perhaps the only one in all that crowd who was not to be deceived and blinded by this scene of universal triumph and delight.

Although the sky was serene she saw the black clouds which were pregnant with storms, and already heard the growling of the thunder that was to shatter, eternally shatter the throne of the Emperor. She knew the day would come, and was not far off, when all these thousands who were now bowing to him would again turn from him and deny him, as they had already done once, and that on that day the triumph of the present hour would be considered a crime! Hortense felt all this, but she did not tremble at her previsions.

The Emperor was in power again, he was the lord and father Josephine had left her, and she must and would be faithful and obedient to him as long as she lived.

And as yet there was no immediate sign of his downfall. Fortune seemed still to smile on him, and in the drawing-room of the Queen, where the diplomatists and statesmen, the artists and officers, of the empire were again assembled, joy and amusement reigned. Literature and music, the arts and sciences, in beateous alliance, rendered it an abode of bliss, where the cup of triumph was emptied to the dregs.

Benjamin Constant, who had changed from a zealous Royalist into an Imperial Councillor of State, came to Hortense's salon and read his novel, "Adolphe," and Talleyrand seemed to have nothing else to do than amuse the Queen and her court by witty anecdotes and new social games.

Labedoyère brought into fashion a number of elegant, idyllic trifles, which became the material for amusement and coquetry among the court ladies. He taught them the poetic language of flowers, and made it the means of communication in the circle that assembled around him. He also invented the alphabet of precious stones, where each different stone represented a certain letter, and in connection with its fellow-gems formed mottos and devices that were mounted on bracelets, necklaces, and rings.

Thus we see that the things with which the court of the Tuileries occupied themselves during the hundred days were of an innocent description.

One evening General Bertrand came to tell

the Queen that the Emperor proposed breakfasting with her next morning at Malmaison. It was ten in the evening, and the preparations had to be made in all haste; but the Queen's head-cook was equal to the occasion. Not so his mistress, however; she feared the effect of revisiting a spot she had not seen since her mother's death.

"I shall not be able to refrain from weeping," she said, "when I find myself at the spot which my brother forced me to leave with a broken heart. The Emperor, who works all day, wishes a moment's distraction, and for him Malmaison only recalls pleasant recollections. I should be wretched if I added bitterness to his pleasure by the sight of my grief, and yet I know not if I shall have sufficient strength to overcome my feelings."

After a moment's reflection the Queen added: "There is only one way; have the horses put to at once, I will sleep at Malmaison; by arriving at night I shall be able to yield to my feelings without fear of troubling anybody, and I shall be all the better to-morrow."

The next day the Emperor arrived, and passed

the breakfast-time in conversing with Denon about the pictures in the Louvre. Presently he rose:

"I should like to see the bed-room of the Empress Josephine," he said, in a voice that betrayed his deep feelings.

The Queen rose in her turn:

"No, Hortense, remain, my daughter, I will go alone, for it would affect you too deeply."

Some time after he returned, and in spite of all his efforts to appear calm, it could easily be seen that he was oppressed, and that a gentle and sad recollection had been aroused in his mind. His eyes were moist, and it seemed as if he desired to wrap himself up in a serious and stern air, in order to escape the weakness which he wished neither to feel nor to display.

CHAPTER IX.

NAPOLEON'S LAST FAREWELL.

THE storm which Queen Hortense had long felt to be approaching was speedily to gather. All the potentates of Europe, who had once been the Emperor's allies, declared themselves against him. There was not one amongst them willing to recognise Napoleon, not one who even condescended to negotiate with him as a sovereign.

"No peace, negotiation, or reconciliation with this man, henceforth," wrote Alexander to Pozzo di Borgo, "all Europe shares my opinion on this point. We wish nothing beyond the fall of this man. France may have what she likes, we will force no sovereign upon her, and the war will be over as soon as this man is removed."

But in order to "remove this man" war became necessary.

The armies of the allied powers at once approached the French frontiers. War was declared against France, or rather against the Emperor Napoleon, and the unhappy country that was longing for peace, and had only consented to the return of the Bourbons in order to secure its blessings, was once more dragged into war.

On the 12th of June the Emperor with his army left Paris to meet his enemies. Napoleon, who formerly had never failed to be cheerful and confident of success, seemed on this occasion to be gloomy, and as if haunted by evil presentiments. He well knew that his all, that his own fate and that of France, depended on this one army. This time there was no question of conquests, it was for national independence, it was for the protection of the French soil, that the war-trumpet was sounded.

Paris, which had seen eighty days of uninterrupted rejoicing, was seized with the spasm of expectation. Music and dancing and shouting ceased; all were listening whether they could not hear the roar of the cannon on the battle-field.

But the days of victory had passed. The cannon *did* roar, a battle was fought, but it was a contest that led to destruction instead of victory.

At Waterloo the eagles, which on the 1st of June had been consecrated and distributed in the Champ-de-Mai, fell into the dust. Without an army, and as a fugitive, the Emperor returned to Paris, while the victorious allies were fast approaching the capital.

Upon the earliest intelligence of Napoleon's return, Hortense hastened to the Elysée, where the Emperor had taken up his quarters, to receive him.

She had been sad and downcast for some days past, a presentiment of evil had haunted her, but now that the misfortune had actually come, now that everybody despaired, she was composed, and ready to stand by the Emperor even to the last.

Napoleon was lost. Hortense knew it; but he stood at that moment more than ever in need of friends, and she remained faithful to him at a time when most of his relations and followers forsook him.

On the 22nd of June the Emperor sent in to the Chambers his abdication in favour of his son, the King of Rome, and on the following day the Prince was proclaimed Emperor of the French, under the name of Napoleon II.

But the new Emperor was a boy of four years of age, and at the time not even in France, but in the hands of his grandfather, the Emperor of Austria, whose armies were even now advancing as enemies towards the capital.

Napoleon had lost his Imperial crown a second time; he was again, and finally, compelled to leave Paris to await the fate his enemies were preparing for him.

This time he did not go to Fontainebleau, but to Malmaison, the place where Josephine had lived after her separation from the Emperor, and where death had overtaken her. The Palace had come into the possession of Hortense, and Napoleon, who but yesterday had possessed power over a vast empire, but who now had nothing he could call his own,—Napoleon asked her permission to go to Malmaison.

Hortense of course received him with open arms. When her friends, who heard of it, hastened to express their regret that she should thus identify her lot, and that of her sons, with the fate of the Emperor, she answered:

"The very danger of the step has led me to take it. I consider it a sacred duty to stand by the Emperor to the very last. The more unfortunate he is, the happier shall I be at having an opportunity for proving to him my devotion and attachment."

One of the Queen's most intimate and devoted friends ventured at this critical moment to remind Hortense what infamous and disgraceful rumours had once been set afloat concerning her relations to Napoleon, and that these rumours had not yet altogether died out. She besought her royal friend not to give calumny a new opportunity for attacking her by receiving the Emperor at Malmaison, but Hortense, too high-minded to be actuated by selfish motives, replied:

"I do not care for these calumnies, and will not allow them to prevent me from the discharge of my duty. The Emperor has always treated me as his child, and I shall therefore never cease being his dutiful and affectionate daughter. The highest aim I strive for is to be at peace with myself."

Hortense therefore went to join the Emperor at Malmaison, where the few who had remained faithful to him assembled to protect him, and lent his residence once more the transient appearance of greatness and splendour. There were marshals and generals, princes and dukes assembled around him to administer to his comfort, and protect his life against the rashness of fanaticism, or the hired dagger of the assassin.

But Napoleon's fate was already decided, and nothing could alter it. When intelligence reached him that the allies were approaching nearer and nearer, that resistance was no longer offered them; when he saw that all was lost, that all had fallen to pieces, his crown and his throne —even the love which he thought he had kindled in the hearts of the French nation by his victories and conquests—he resolved to flee. Whither he cared but little: his only object was to leave the country that had forsaken him.

The Emperor resolved to go to Rochefort, and thence return to the island of Elba. The provisional government that had been formed in Paris, and had sent a messenger to Malmaison to request the Emperor to depart immediately, commissioned this gentleman to accompany Napoleon, and not to leave him until his embarkation had taken place.

One of the most glaring instances of ingratitude displayed at this period was shown by Marshal Davoust, at that period minister of war and commander-in-chief of the army, one of the generals on whom the Emperor had lavished his kindness, for his revenues amounted to 1,800,000 francs a year. Napoleon sent his aide-de-camp, General de Flahault, to this man, to obtain for him a respite of twenty hours from the provisional government; but his reply was:

"Tell *your* Bonaparte that if he does not start at once I shall go and compel him."

General de Flahault felt so indignant at the reply that he broke his sword, and gave in his resignation to the marshal; then he turned his back on him, adding, that he would consider himself dishonoured if he served under such a man any longer. It is to be hoped that the Emperor never learned the insult offered him by a lieutenant to whom he had ever been deeply attached.

Napoleon was willing to depart. He was to start on the afternoon of the 30th of June. All that was left for him to do was to take leave of his friends and his family. He did it with a tearless eye; his features were cold and immovable, even to hardness.

It was only when Hortense entered the room, when for the last time he clasped her boys in his arms, that an expression of pain passed over his face, and his lips trembled: he turned away; perhaps it was to conceal a tear.

When after a while he again faced Hortense to bid her farewell too, his countenance was as stern and harsh as before. Hortense knew well what a tempest of feelings there was in that breast.

The Queen now asked him to grant her a last favour.

A sarcastic smile moved for a moment the rigid features of the Emperor. So he was yet able to give something? There was a favour left which it was in his power to grant? With a motion of his head he nodded consent.

Hortense gave him a large black bandage.

"Sire," she said, "wear this bandage round your body. Conceal it carefully, but in time of need open it."

The Emperor took the bandage; he was surprised at its great weight.

"What does it contain?" he asked, "I wish to know."

"Sire," Hortense replied, blushing, and with a faltering voice, "it is my large diamond necklace. I have taken it to pieces and sewed the stones up. Your Majesty may one day be so situated as to require some money. I hope you will not deprive me of the satisfaction of knowing that my last gift was accepted."

The Emperor at first refused, but Hortense was so persevering in her entreaties that he at last consented to accept his stepdaughter's present.

Then they exchanged a few hurried words of parting, and Hortense, in order to hide the tears that were rushing into her eyes, hastened to leave the apartments with her boys.

Napoleon rang the bell, and gave orders that nobody should be admitted into his apartments, but at the very moment when the order was being given the door opened and a national guard entered.

"Talma!" the Emperor exclaimed in an almost cheerful tone, "you here?"

And he stretched out his hand to the man who had just entered.

"Yes, Talma, sire," the visitor replied, pressing the Emperor's hand to his lips. "I have come here in this disguise to bid your Majesty good-bye."

"It is a good-bye for ever, Talma!" replied Napoleon; "I shall never again admire you in your great characters. I am about to set out on a journey from which I shall never return. You will be an emperor for many an evening yet, but it is different with me! My part is played out, Talma."

"No, sire. You will never cease to be the Emperor!" Talma replied enthusiastically; "although you possess no crown and no purple."

"And no people," the Emperor added.

"Sire, you have a people, and will always have one. You sit on a throne that will never fall. It is the throne you have built yourself on the battle-field, and which will be remembered in the

annals of history.   He who reads your life, to
whatever nation he may belong, will bow to the
Emperor."

"I have no people, Talma!   They have all forsaken me, they have all betrayed me."

"Sire, the day must come when they will regret it ; and Alexander of Russia, too, will regret
having forsaken the great man he once called his
brother."

It was Talma's generous wish to remind the
Emperor in this hour of humiliation of his former
victories, in order that this remembrance might
give him strength.   He continued :

"Does your Majesty recollect that evening at
Erfurt, when the Emperor of Russia, in the presence of everybody and to the admiration of the
audience, made you such a striking declaration of
friendship? Oh, you will have forgotten it, sire! For
you it was an event of common occurrence, but I
shall never forget it.   It was in the theatre.   We
were playing 'Œdipus.'   I looked up to the box
in which you were sitting, between the King of
Würtemberg and the Emperor of Russia.   I had
eyes for none but you, the second Alexander of
Macedon, the second Cæsar, and raised my arms

towards you, when, true to my character, I had
to say: *L'amitié d'un grand homme est un bienfait
des Dieux.* And as I spoke thus, Alexander rose
and embraced you. I saw it, and tears prevented
me from continuing to speak. The audience burst
into enthusiastic applause; but it was not intended
for me, it was in honour of the Emperor Alexander."

Whilst Talma was thus speaking with spark-
ling eye and glowing cheek, a gentle smile passed
over the pallid features of the Emperor. Talma
had gained his object, he had succeeded in con-
soling the humiliated Emperor by the recollection
of his former greatness.

Napoleon thanked him with a kindly look, and
stretched out his hand in a last farewell.

Talma was just about leaving the room, when
a carriage drove up. It was the carriage destined
to take away the Emperor.

At this moment the door opened, and a tall,
majestic-looking woman entered the room, whose
noble and almost classical features were half hidden by grey curls.

It was Lætitia, the Emperor's mother, who
had come once more to see her son. Talma, in

breathless excitement, stood immovable, and con-
gratulated himself upon being permitted to witness so interesting a scene.

Napoleon's mother passed Talma without no-
ticing him. She saw nothing but her son, who
stood in the middle of the room, fixing his gaze
with an indescribable expression on his parent.

They stood opposite each other, mother and
son. The Emperor's countenance remained un-
changed and immovable, it seemed as if fate had
converted him into a marble statue of himself.

For a while they stood opposite each other
without speaking. Two large tears rolled down
Lætitia's cheek. Talma, who was standing in the
back-ground, wept bitterly, but Napoleon showed
no sign of emotion.

At length Lætitia raised both her hands, and
stretching them out to the Emperor, said with a
clear and sonorous voice :

"Farewell, my son !"

Napoleon pressed her hands in his, and looked
long and affectionately in her face. Then with a
voice as firm as his mother's had been, he exclaimed :

"Farewell, my mother !"

Once more they looked at each other. The Emperor let his mother's hand fall; Lœtitia turned to depart, and at the same moment General Bertrand entered to announce that all was ready for leaving Malmaison.

We may be allowed to interpolate a few words here about Madame Lœtitia, and describe some traits which honour her character and her sex. After the defection of Murat, which did so much injury to the French army, and was the principal cause of their misfortune, Madame Mère broke off all relations with her daughter, the Queen of Naples. The attempts the latter made to effect a reconciliation were in vain; but at last she found her way in, and presented herself to Madame, with the affection and tenderness of a daughter who came to ask her mother what she had done to merit such treatment. Queen Caroline received the following reply:

"What you have done, good Heavens! You betrayed your brother, your benefactor."

The Queen of Naples remarked, with some degree of justice, that her husband was alone master of his policy, that imperious circumstances and the interests of his kingdom necessitated his rupture with France, and that no one, much less her mother, could find a culprit in her.

"You betrayed your benefactor," Madame Mère repeated, "you should have employed all your influence with your husband to turn him from his fatal resolution. Murat ought to have passed over your dead body before committing such a felonious act; the Emperor was no less his benefactor than yours: retire, Caroline."

And she turned her back on her. It was not till after the Emperor's death that Madame Lætitia became reconciled to her daughter.

In 1820, when a Bonapartist conspiracy was denounced to the Chambers of Paris; when Spain rose, through the courage of the illustrious and unfortunate Riego; when Naples revolted, and all Italy was covered by Carbonari—the government of the Bourbons felt great alarm. Deceived by false information, it appealed to the Pope against the behaviour of Madame Lætitia, who was then residing at Rome. She had, it was stated, her agents in Corsica to foment there an insurrection in favour of Napoleon, that its ramifications extended into the interior of France, to gain partizans for her son, and that the king was aware of

the number of millions Madame Lætitia employed
for all this. In the eyes of any man of common
sense these stupid accusations fell of themselves,
and it was more than absurd to suspect a woman
of Madame Mère's age, who was close upon eighty,
who never left her home or received a stranger,
and was only visited at intervals by those of her
family who resided in Rome, and daily by her
brother, the Cardinal. It was really atrocious to
impute such designs to the Emperor's mother,
and point her out as the first mover in a conspiracy, but the Duke de Blacas represented the
King of France at Rome, and the hatred he bore
the members of the Imperial family permitted no
doubt about his being the author of so ridiculous
a fable.

A very grave complaint was addressed on this
subject by M. de Blacas to the Papal government.
The Pope, when he heard it, ordered his Secre-
tary of State to proceed to Madame Lætitia and
make an inquiry into this matter. His Eminence
proceeded to Madame Mère, and explained to her
the motive of his visit in the fullest details.
After expressing his regret at being compelled to
undertake so painful a mission, he brought to

her knowledge the charges France had made against her.

Madame Lætitia, who allowed him to speak without interruption, heard him to the end, and then replied with dignity:

"Monsieur le Cardinal, I have no millions, but be good enough to tell the Pope, in order that my remarks may be repeated to King Louis XVIII., that were I fortunate enough to possess the fortune so charitably attributed to me, I should not employ it in fomenting troubles in Corsica, or to secure my son partizans in France, for he has enough of them; but I should use it to equip a fleet with a special mission, that of proceeding to fetch the Emperor from St Helena, where the most infamous and dishonourable conduct keeps him prisoner."

Then, bowing to the Cardinal, she withdrew to her private apartments.

We will now return to the Emperor, who hurried to Rochefort, having with him in the carriage General Beckert, the commissary appointed by the Provisional Government to accompany him till he embarked. On his arrival at Rochefort the Emperor found there his brother Joseph, who was about to embark on board an American ship and proceed to the United States, which he succeeded in doing.

A Danish captain, whose vessel was reputed to be an excellent sailer, and who happened to be lying in La Rochelle roads, offered to convey the Emperor to New York, and answered for the success of the enterprise with his head : but he insisted on a special condition ; it was that the Emperor should embark alone, and hide himself in a secret berth, which he refused to do.

There was one way of saving the Emperor from the English cruisers, and the attachment his brother Joseph bore him was a guarantee that this infallible way would not have been proposed in vain. All that was necessary was for Joseph to assume the grey coat and hat, and, surrounded by the Emperor's friends, allow himself to be captured by the English. Certainly the resemblance in the face was striking, and there was not so much difference in the height of the two brothers as to allow the ingenious stratagem to be detected. The English once holding Joseph as prisoner, would have hurried with him to Portsmouth, and the Emperor could have proceeded to

America with the greater facility, as the British squadron would have been withdrawn.

Mdlle. de Cochelet frequently conversed with the Queen on this subject, and they were quite agreed as to its feasibility.

"If the Emperor or his brother had hit on the idea," the Queen said, "it would have been a bright page in Joseph's history : and from my knowledge of him I do not think he would have allowed the opportunity for such an act of devotion to slip."

CHAPTER X.

THE BANISHMENT OF THE QUEEN.

So soon as the Emperor had finally departed, everybody began asking himself,—What king shall we have? assuredly it cannot be one of the Bourbons; after having been thus expelled, how could it be possible for them to return? Prince Eugène was the popular favourite, but all joined in the cry of "No more. Bourbons!"

Fouché himself wrote to the foreign ministers that it was hopeless to dream of bringing back the Bourbons; that the Revolution of '89 could not be effaced, and attempting to go beyond it would be the way to bring it back. No stability could be hoped for, save with the new dynasty, and the Regency was best fitted for France, because it represented the principles of the Revolution, and gave the institutions time to be established on the wide basis which the wants of the country demanded.

On July 1st many officers of the army spent the evening with the Queen, having left their quarters without obtaining leave. General Excelmans and Colonels Lascour and Lawoestine did not conceal their despair at the departure of the Emperor, and made the Queen a proposition which could only have emanated from that despair.

"Come with us, Madame," they said to her; "withdraw to the heart of that army among whom you and yours count sincerely devoted friends: we shall be too happy to watch over you and your children, and escort you till you have reached a place of safety; each regiment in turn will act as your guard, and feel proud of the privilege."

The Queen was deeply affected by their offer, but did not hesitate about declining it.

"I am not in a position to form such a resolution," she said to them, with her ordinary gentleness, " I must undergo my fate : I am no longer anything, I cannot produce the belief that I am rallying the troops round me, or change their destination in order to protect myself. Had I been sovereign of France, I would have done everything in the world for defence. I gave the same advice to my sister the Empress Marie Louise in 1814. I would not have left the capital until it became utterly impossible to save it ; then and only then I would have retired among you : but it is not for me to mingle my destiny with such mighty interests as those of France, and I must resign myself to isolation, to persecutions, perhaps, which I have certainly not merited."

" But what do you intend to do, Madame ?" General Excelmans asked.

" Quit Paris and France for ever—Europe, if it be necessary, so soon as I have my passports and the roads are free to enable me to travel in safety."

" Reflect carefully on this, Madame, you are alone and your children so young. It is really alarming."

" I know it, General, but what is to be done ?

I will proceed to a country where I may be able to live in peace—to Switzerland, America, no matter where, provided that I am far from the agitations of the world, and sheltered from the events which are about to overthrow so many destinies."

Such were the last marks of devotion offered the Queen, which her good sense and resignation did not allow her to avail herself of, as she did not wish to associate any one in her misfortunes, or prolong, for her private interests, a struggle already so alarming for the country.

The hope of defending Paris, which had so long been kept up, faded away. People had believed that Marshal Davoust, who had so frequently distinguished himself, and in the last instance by the defence of Hamburg, would give a second display of his skill in Paris, but he had grown old and demanded rest. This was the reason he had not commanded a *corps d'armée* during the last short campaign. Napoleon had employed his talent in the Ministry of War. Davoust, moreover, was uncomfortable in his private life, for his wife was suffering greatly. These circumstances seemed to have exercised an influence over him: and though he was Com-

mander-in-chief of the army under the walls of
Paris, he was subordinate to the Provisional
Government.

The Queen was repeatedly insulted by the
hired agents of the Faubourg St Germain, and resolved to retire to a place of safety, but an inci-
dent delayed her departure. The inhabitants of
St Leu had resisted the allied troops, and one of
the gamekeepers was taken by the Prussians and
sentenced to be shot. The Queen's first object
was to save this man, and she applied to Prince
William of Prussia, who interceded and saved
him.

On July 4th the Convention sending the
French army beyond the Loire was signed, and
the capital surrendered defencelessly to the allies.
The Provisional Government resigned *en masse*,
alleging that the allies had not fulfilled their promise of allowing the French nation to select their
own monarch. When the Queen heard this she
said to Mademoiselle de Cochelet,—

"Good Heaven! is it possible that an assembly
of sensible men, whose intentions are good, should
have deceived themselves so grossly about the
position of France? Make speeches, send envoys

to an enemy who does not receive them ! Imagine that incredible forces have marched upon France only to see what the nation decided on, adopted —it is incredible ! The Emperor was quite right when he said, a few days ago, at Malmaison, with an undefinable expression of sorrow, 'We have fallen back into the lower Empire, and people amuse themselves with coolly discoursing, when the enemy is at the gates.'"

On July 3rd Louis XVIII. made his triumphal entry into Paris. It was the more brilliant be-cause the mob was composed of Dukes, Mar-quises, and Counts: quality was substituted for quantity. The exultation was delirious, the cries and gestures became convulsive, so suffocating was the joy of the dominant party. The hand-some equipages of elegant ladies encumbered the passage of the sovereign surnamed *le Désiré*; they passed incessantly, waving their white hand-kerchiefs, people shook hands from the carriage windows, and to set the seal on the whole, a great lady, whose equipage was standing on the Boule-vard de Gand, took her coachman round the neck and embraced him convulsively.

For the second time the Bourbons entered
Paris with the aid of foreign bayonets; Louis
XVIII. was once more King of France. But
this time he did not come with mild and concilia-
tory intentions. He came to punish and to reward, but mercy was not to be found in his
train.

The old generals and marshals of the empire,
who had been unable to resist the call of their
former master, were now deprived of their rank,
exiled or shot. Both Ney and Labedoyère had
to pay with their lives for their generous attachment to the Emperor, and all who had been connected with the Napoleon family were treated
with the utmost harshness and severity.

The calumnies which in 1814 had been sowed
against Hortense, were now to bring forth melancholy fruit. They resembled the dragon's teeth
that sprung up into hostile warriors, and these
warriors on the present occasion attacked a defenceless woman.

Louis XVIII. had returned to the throne of
his fathers, but he had not yet forgotten what
they had told him on his road to Holland, that it

was all the doing of the Duchess of St Leu, and her intrigues alone had brought back the Emperor.

Now that Louis was King once more he remembered this, and wished to have his revenge. He asked it as a favour of the Emperor Alexander not to visit the Duchess de St Leu this time.

The Emperor was startled at the strange rumours that were in circulation about Hortense. He had already begun to be under the mysterious influence of Madame de Krüdener, who turned him away from the world; he did as the Bourbons wished, and gave the Queen up.

This was the signal for the Royalists to throw off all restraint in the gratification of their jealousy and hatred of Hortense. They were now at full liberty to deride and calumniate her in the meanest manner, and eagerly seized the opportunity for doing so. They now meant to have their revenge for having been compelled to bow to Hortense as to a Queen. Their dastardly attacks were carried to an incredible height. Was not the woman whom they insulted the step-daughter of Napoleon? Their very cowardice became a merit in the eyes of the royal family, for to slander and persecute the Napoleon family was loving and flattering the Bourbons.

The Royalists never abandoned their victim for a single moment. Hortense was a hateful memento of the empire, and for that reason she must be removed, like the statue on the Place Vendôme.

Whilst the poor Queen was sitting lonely and sad in the remotest part of her hôtel, the rumour was spread by the Royalists that she was plotting again, and that in the dusk of evening she would leave her house to harangue the people and excite them to rebellion. It was a positive fact, they said, that she advised them, if not to demand back the Emperor, at least to insist upon the little king of Rome ascending the throne instead of a Bourbon.

When Mademoiselle de Cochelet, the Queen's faithful companion and friend, acquainted her mistress with the existence of these rumours, the Queen took but little notice of it.

"Why, Madame," exclaimed Mademoiselle de Cochelet, "you listen to it as quietly as if I were relating the history of the last century."

"It is indeed the same to me," Hortense replied quietly; "all is lost for us, and I look upon the worst that can now happen to me with the indifference of a spectator. I consider it perfectly natural that people should be anxious to defame me, for I bear a name at whose sound the world has trembled, and which will continue to be a great one, whatever they may do to us. But I must take measures to protect myself and children against this hatred. I mean to leave France and retire to Switzerland, where on the banks of the Lake of Geneva I possess a small estate."

But the Queen was not even allowed to make the necessary preparations for her voyage. The Royalists had succeeded in thoroughly poisoning the King's mind against Hortense, and as the Government was afraid of the helpless woman and her two little boys, they hastened to get rid of them as soon as possible.

Early on the 17th of July an aide-de-camp of the Prussian General, Müffling, who was then the military commandant of Paris, called at the house of the Duchess de St Leu, and told her steward that within two hours she must leave the capital. It was not without difficulty Monsieur Deveaux obtained permission for his mistress to remain six hours. Hortense was obliged to submit to the order. She was compelled to leave Paris without having been able to arrange her affairs and make the necessary preparations. Her only moveable fortune consisted in her precious stones, and these, of course, she intended taking with her. But in an official warning she was told that a band of fanatic Royalists had heard of her departure, and had left Paris to waylay her, in order "to strip her of those millions she tried to carry off."

The Duchess was advised not to attempt, under such circumstances, taking with her much money or other valuables, but only to provide herself with what was absolutely necessary.

At the same time General Müffling offered her an escort of Prussian troops, which, however, was refused. Hortense only asked that an Austrian officer might be allowed to accompany her to protect them on their journey. Her request was granted, and Count Voyna, the aide-de-camp of Prince Schwarzenberg, was intrusted with this delicate mission.

They set out on their journey on the evening of the 17th of July, 1815. Hortense's faithful

11 *

companion, Mademoiselle de Cochelet, remained
in Paris to settle her mistress's affairs and secure
her diamonds. Accompanied only by her equery,
Monsieur de Marmold, Count Voyna, her children, a maid, and a footman, the Queen left Paris
to proceed into exile.

Hortense's journey through her beloved
France, to which she had ceased to belong, was
a sad and melancholy one. The country that had
once adored the Emperor and his family seemed
now animated by an intense hatred against them.

All Bonapartists remained during these days
of excitement in their hiding-places, or at least
carefully concealed their true political colour behind the mask of Bourbonism. Thus it came
about that only Royalists were to be met with
in Hortense's way, and they fancied they could
not evince their loyalty in any better manner
than by assaulting a poor, defenceless woman, and
greeting her with derision, insults, and maledictions, simply because she bore the name that was
once idolized by France, although the legitimists
had never ceased to hate it.

More than once was her Austrian protector
compelled to defend her and her children against

the furious attacks of Royalist bands, upon her own countrymen. At Dijon, Count Voyna was even forced to call out the Austrian garrison, in order to protect the Duchess against a fanatic mob, which was led and excited by royal guards and noble ladies ornamented with white lilies.

Broken in spirit by what she had been obliged to see and experience, downcast and despairing, Hortense at last arrived in Geneva. But the thought that she would at length find here solitude and peace consoled her. She retired at once to her small estate on the banks of the lake, which bears the name of Pregny.

Hortense was not allowed, however, to enjoy her place of refuge long. The French ambassador to Switzerland, who was residing in Geneva, told the municipal authorities that his government would not suffer the Queen to settle so near the French frontier, and demanded her immediate departure. The authorities of Geneva obeyed, and ordered Hortense at once to quit the town.

When Count Voyna brought the Duchess this bad piece of news, and asked her where she intended going now, she exclaimed despairingly :

"I do not know where to go! Throw me in the lake, then we shall all be at rest!"

But she soon recovered her usual proud self-possession, and submitted patiently to the new exile, which deprived her of her last possession, the charming little estate of Pregny, her *rêve de bonheur*.

In Aix she was at last allowed to live in peace for a few weeks. It was in this town she had once enjoyed proud triumphs, and now she was suffered at least to exist with her children and a few servants within its walls.

But at Aix she was to receive the severest blow Fate had ever yet dealt her.

So far back as 1814, and shortly before the Emperor's return, she had lost the law-suit against her husband, and been condemned to give up to him her eldest son, Napoleon Louis. Now that Napoleon's displeasure was no longer to be feared, Louis demanded that this verdict should be carried out, and sent a Baron de Zuyten to fetch the boy away and remove him to Florence, where his father was then living.

It was no longer in the power of the unhappy mother to resist the claims of her husband. She was obliged to submit, and allow the boy to be taken to a father who was a stranger to him, and for whom therefore his heart could not feel any affection.

The scene of parting between mother and son was a heart-rending one, and little Louis, who had never been separated from his brother for a moment, wept bitterly, and throwing his arms round his neck, besought him not to go away.

But the separation had become imperative. Hortense, herself, tore the two boys from each other, and clasped little Louis Napoleon to her bosom, whilst Napoleon, bathed in tears, followed his tutor to the carriage. When Hortense heard it roll away she fainted and sank to the ground. A long and serious illness was the consequence of this separation.

CHAPTER XI.

THE AUTHOR OF THE HOLY ALLIANCE.

WE have seen that Mademoiselle de Cochelet
remained in Paris after the Queen's departure,
to watch over her mistress's private affairs, and
save what she could out of the wreck. While
thus engaged she heard of the arrival in Paris of
Madame de Krüdener, and hurried to assure
herself of the help of this friend at Court.

Madame de Krüdener was residing at Altorf
when the war broke out, and the hostile armies
passed through that town in succession; she was
still there when the Russian troops arrived and

indulged in the most revolting excesses. A poor family, in which Madame de Krüdener took an interest, were most shamefully beaten and maltreated, and Madame de Krüdener in her grief resolved to apply to Alexander directly; she, therefore, proceeded to his head-quarters, and asked him to stop the excesses of his troops, predicting that if he did not maintain discipline and order in his army God would not bless his enterprise.

Without any introduction or letter of recommendation she presented herself to the Emperor Alexander, and was greatly surprised at being received immediately on mentioning her name. Madame de Krüdener found the Emperor alone, and he showed her the greatest attention.

"It is the hand of God that brings you here, Madame," he said, "at a moment when I ardently desired your presence, and was asking Heaven to enlighten me with reference to its designs about me."

He then told her that his wife, whom she had seen the previous year at Baden Baden, had spoken to him a good deal about her; that he was aware of all that Madame de Krüdener had

said to the Empress, which had struck him, but
he was more surprised at seeing all the events
she had predicted realized; that he incessantly
thought about it, and that at the very moment
when he was interrupted by the announcement
of her visit, he was praying for enlightenment
and for her arrival.

As this extraordinary coincidence could only
appear to the Emperor a miracle, he was quite
convinced of Madame de Krüdener's celestial
mission, and the counsels she gave him as to the
duties of his position, and the necessity of con-
ciliation, protection, and peace so affected him,
that from this moment he would not permit her
to leave him again, and never let a day pass without seeing her.

Madame de Krüdener proceeded to Paris with
the staff, and arrived there on the same day as
Alexander; she took up her quarters in a house
not far from the Elysée Bourbon, where the Emperor resided.   Every evening he skirted the
gardens of the Faubourg St Honoré, and, followed by only one Cossack, joined Madame de
Krüdener by a back gate, where he prayed with

her, and revived his confidence and faith by the
lady's exhortations. They passed several hours
together, during which no one was admitted to
Madame de Krüdener, and the Emperor's household supposed him to be at work in his cabinet.

Madame de Krüdener spoke to Mademoiselle
de Cochelet about the Queen with all the interest and affection she felt for her, and again
repeated that the Emperor Alexander could alone
efficaciously protect her.

"I know," she said, "that he is not as well
disposed towards the Queen as he formerly was;
he believes that she has interfered in politics, and
is angry with her on that account, but this cloud
will pass over, for he is too good, too noble, too
generous,—his is a soul worthy of Heaven. I
must insist on your seeing the Emperor Alexander,
and it will be easy for you to have an explanation
with him. Come to me at the time when he
pays me his usual visit, and I guarantee to procure you a kind reception."

At first Mademoiselle de Cochelet declined
this offer, through fear of compromising the
Queen, but by the inducement of the Duke de

Vicenza, who pointed out how much Hortense required a protector, she consented to see the Emperor.

A great change had taken place in a year; formerly the Emperor would call in Mademoiselle de Cochelet, and over a dish of tea talk about the future of the Queen of Holland. Now, the Emperor was stern and conscious of his dignity. Madame de Krüdener was the first to break the embarrassing silence, by saying she believed that he would not be sorry to see an old acquaintance, against whom he had been unfairly prejudiced.

Mademoiselle de Cochelet then said that if the Emperor's unfavourable opinions had been confined to herself, she would not have thought herself worthy of the attempt to dissipate them, but as they extended to the Queen, she thought it her duty to do her utmost to induce the Emperor to do her mistress the justice she deserved.

"I still feel my old friendship for Queen Hortense," he replied, "but I frankly confess that I do not like ladies to interfere in politics, and on that head the Queen has been altogether different from what I supposed."

"But, sire, what has she done that does not agree with the qualities and character your Majesty was pleased to recognise in her? for there are positions in which ladies are compelled to take part in political events."

"Assuredly: but, after receiving, from the kindness of the King of France, permission to remain at Paris, the Queen ought not to have mingled so actively as she did in politics."

"Say, from *your* kindness, sire, for you cannot have forgotten that the Queen would receive nothing from the Bourbons, and that she only yielded to your wishes in accepting what you offered her."

"No matter from whom she accepted favour, she ought not to have remained in Paris when the Emperor Napoleon returned."

"I know not what she ought to have done from a political point of view, but as daughter and sister of the Emperor, her duty ever was superior to her interests, and if the Queen fulfilled it actively it was not in the moment of triumph, but when misfortune arrived, by proceeding to Malmaison to share the dangers of a man to whom she owed everything, watching over his safety, and softening the humiliations of the last days of the crisis."

"That character was fully worthy of Queen Hortense," the Emperor said, giving up the dry tone he had hitherto assumed, " and if I could be useful to her in any matter, I would do so willingly."

Unhappily for the Queen, her companion was constrained to exercise a reserve, and she merely replied:

" It will surely be very agreeable, sire, to the Queen to hear of the interest your Majesty still takes in her, but as for receiving a service from any one, or having recourse to the protection of any man, no matter who he may be, she has clearly proved that this was not her intention by leaving Paris as she has done. She had scarcely the time to procure necessaries, and was unable to take her jewels with her, which now constitute her sole fortune, and which she would not expose to the risks of travelling."

"I am vexed that under the circumstances she did not think of applying to me, and if you wish to send her her jewels, I will have them delivered by a sure hand."

"I thank your Majesty, but I have deposited the precious objects belonging to the Queen in safety. For the moment she does not require them; a set of rubies and diamonds which she has commissioned me to dispose of will supply her with the means of existence for some time to come."

"The Emperor still pressed Mademoiselle de Cochelet, but she did not dare accept any favour in her mistress's name. The set of rubies and diamonds was sold at one-fourth its value, as were most of the articles belonging to the Queen, but the person with whom Mademoiselle de Cochelet deposited the proceeds became bankrupt. The Emperor Alexander had an opportunity for obliging Hortense and Eugène soon after. Several fine pictures, left at Malmaison, and given by Napoleon to Josephine, were the result of conquest. The Elector of Hesse Cassel demanded them, and to prevent his getting hold of them, Alexander had them conveyed to his palace, and paid their value to the brother and sister.

Madame de Krüdener, strange to say, did not exert her undoubted influence to save any victims from the reaction that set in. She could have done so easily, but doubtless attached no value to their perishable bodies, and contented herself with praying for their souls.

To her too was owing the idea of the Holy Alliance. One evening, when Mademoiselle de Cochelet visited her, she told her friend how she had been exhorting the Emperor Alexander to raise the banner of Christ.

"The reign of the Saviour will come, sire," she said to him; "glory and happiness for those who fought for Him! Maledictions and woe on those who fought against Him! Form a Holy Alliance of all those who belong to the true faith, and let them take an oath to combat the innovators, who wish to overthrow religion, and you will triumph eternally with it."

The Emperor Alexander may have listened to this advice, but it is quite certain that, when he reviewed his army in Champagne, he insisted on Madame de Krüdener accompanying him, and inspecting the battalions. As no man in the world more feared ridicule than did the Emperor of Russia, to brave it as he did by thus displaying his relations with Madame de Krüdener needed a firm conviction on his part. For age, the face of the inspired prophetess, and her grey hair, allowed no misinterpretation of the motives that actuated him.

This extraordinary woman came to a bad end: she committed the fatal mistake of rendering herself ridiculous and an object of suspicion to the police. She eventually died in the Crimea in 1824, her last companion in exile being the Countess of Lamothe, who had been publicly whipped and branded on the Place de Grève at Paris, as the instigator of the notorious robbery of Marie Antoinette's diamond necklace.

CHAPTER XI.

THE CHILDHOOD OF LOUIS NAPOLEON.

ON reaching Aix, the Queen hired the first house
vacant; it was badly situated, gloomy and ugly;
the only advantage it offered being a rather
large court-yard, where the children could play at
their ease. Two or three boys, of about their
own age, joined them, belonging to persons who
lived in the neighbourhood. They played at
soldiers, and the younger Prince, proud of being at
the head and beating the drum, which formed part
of Louis' playthings, drummed away furiously,
making the greatest noise possible, which, how-

ever, could not be heard a very great distance. Prince Napoleon, as the elder and more intelligent, commanded the troop, and drew his little sabre. He dressed the line and raised his voice to its full pitch as he gave the word of command. Prince Louis, armed with a stick like the rest, watched every movement of his brother, who was his model and his idol.

Seated at the window, the Queen and Mademoiselle de Cochelet watched their innocent amusements, little suspecting that they would presently give rise to Police reports—for who would have guessed such aberrations of the human mind?

Even at Aix the unfortunate Queen was not to enjoy a peaceful retirement for long. The Bourbons, who continued to persecute Hortense, but at the same time afraid of the name she bore, although its great representative was banished to a distant isle, considered it dangerous that the Emperor's step-daughter and her son Louis Napoleon (whose very name reminded them of the past) should remain so near to the French frontier. They therefore lodged a protest with the Government of Savoy against the Queen's resi-

dence in that country, and Hortense was compelled once more to move and wander through
the world in search of a home.

She first went to Baden, the Grand-duchess
Stephanie being a near relation of hers, and from
her husband she might therefore well expect a
friendly reception.

But the Grand-duke did not justify the hopes
of his cousin. He had not sufficient courage to
defy the cowardly apprehensions of France. It
was only after persevering entreaties on the part
of his wife, that he at last permitted Hortense to
settle in the furthest corner of his country, in
Constance on the banks of the Lake; but the
Duchess de St Leu had to pledge herself that
neither she nor her son should ever come to
Karlsruhe, and his wife, Stephanie, was obliged to
promise that she would never go to see her cousin
in Constance.

Hortense submitted to these conditions. She
was glad to have found at last a place where she
might rest her weary head. She was tired of
wandering about, and longed to cicatrize the
wounds of her bleeding heart in the silence and
sacred peace of a lovely and sweet locality. At

Constance Hortense spent a few happy years, wishing for nothing and asking for nothing, save a little peace and solitude; her consolation consisted in her son, who reconciled her to all her misfortunes, and whom she intended bringing up to be a strong-minded, energetic man. How she succeeded the world now knows to its ·amazement.

She bestowed the greatest possible care on the education of her son. She engaged a distinguished man, Professor Lebas of Paris, to be the tutor of the young prince, while she herself instructed him in drawing, music, and dancing. She would read and sing with him, and become a child again, to occupy for the lonely, isolated boy the place of the companion he had lost.

When in the long winter evenings she reclined on her couch near the fireside, the boy being on a foot-stool at her feet, she would tell him of his great uncle and his achievements, of France, their dear native country, which at present was closed against them; but to return to which must always be their dearest wish, their most energetic endeavour.

The boy's heart would then swell with enthu-

siasm, when he heard of the great battles his
uncle had won in Italy and Egypt, on the banks
of the Rhine, and on those of the Danube. And
the quiet, pale lad, with his dark, thoughtful eyes,
listened to her in breathless suspense, and his
slender frame trembled with excitement and emotion when he heard what love the Emperor had
borne to France, and how every grand and noble
action he had achieved had only been accomplished for her glory and honour.

One day when the boy was thus sitting at his
mother's feet, pale and breathless with excitement, listening to her stories of the past, Hortense pointed to that beautiful picture, painted by
David, representing Napoleon at the top of the
Alps, the idea for which originated with the
Emperor himself.

"Paint me quietly sitting on a fiery horse,"
Napoleon said to David, and David had taken
the advice. He represented the Emperor on his
charger, rearing proudly on the summit of a rock
that bears the inscriptions "Hannibal" and
"Cæsar." The expression of Napoleon's face is
calm, but his eyes have an unfathomable lustre.
The breeze toys with his hair, and he is unmind-

ful of his rearing steed, whose reins he tightly grasps.

There was a copy of this celebrated painting in the *salon* of the Duchess. She was pointing to it, whilst engaged in relating the Emperor's passage over the Alps, which none but Hannibal and Cæsar had ventured before, and no other perhaps would do after him. The boy's face was radiant with enthusiasm as he listened with intense excitement to his mother's words. He rose, and proudly standing erect, exclaimed:—

"Mother, I too shall cross the Alps one day, like the Emperor."

And whilst he thus spoke, his cheek burned, his lips trembled, and his heart beat audibly.

Hortense felt alarmed. She turned to her companion, Mademoiselle de Cochelet, and begged her, in a whisper, to divert the boy's thoughts by telling him some amusing story. The lady was thinking what story she might choose, when her eye fell on a tea-cup, standing on the mantelpiece. She rose, took the cup, and returned with it to little Louis Napoleon.

"Mamma has explained you a serious picture, Louis," Mademoiselle de Cochelet began;

"now I will show you an amusing one. Look here, is not this very pretty?"

The little prince gave a careless, hasty look at the cup, and nodded his head. Mademoiselle laughed.

"Look here, Louis, this is exactly the opposite to the picture of the Emperor Napoleon riding across the Alps, and meeting the great spirits of Hannibal and Cæsar. This picture represents a little Napoleon, who, instead of ascending the Alps, is descending from his bed, and meets a black ghost in the shape of a little chimney-sweep. This is the story of the little Napoleon. The great Napoleon meets Hannibal, and the small one meets a chimney-sweep."

"Am I the little Napoleon?" the boy inquired.

"Yes, Louis, you are," was the reply, "and now I will tell you the story of the cup. One day, when we were still living in Paris, and your uncle was Emperor of France, you met in your room a poor little chimney-sweep, who in his black dress had just crept out of the chimney. You began crying, for you were frightened, and wished to run away, but I held you fast, and told you that the parents

of these little boys were so poor as to be unable to keep their children at home, but were
compelled to send them to Paris, where at the
risk of their lives they had to gain a livelihood
by creeping into dirty chimneys to clean them.
My description affected you, and you promised
not to be any more afraid of little chimney-
sweeps.

"Some time after you were one morning awakened by a strange noise. Your brother lay sleeping by your side, and the nurse had gone out of
the room. The noise originated with a chimney-
sweep who had just descended, and soon stood
in the middle of the room. On seeing him you
remembered what I had told you, and got out of
bed to hasten to the chair on which your clothes
were lying. You took your purse from the
pocket of your coat, which contained the money
you used to take with you in your walks in order
to give alms, and emptied its contents into the
sooty hand of the chimney-sweep; after this you
wished to return to your bed, but unfortunately it
proved too high for you. On seeing this, the
little chimney-sweep took up the little prince in
his arms to lift him into bed. At this moment

the nurse returned, and your brother, whom the
noise had awakened, began crying terribly at
seeing little Louis in the black arms of the
chimney-sweep.

"This is the story of little Napoleon and the
chimney-sweep. Your grandmamma, the Empress
Josephine, was so amused at it, that your mamma,
wishing agreeably to surprise the Empress, had
this scene painted on a tea-cup which was presented to Josephine. And would you believe it,
Louis, this cup was the means of saving your
cousin, the little King of Rome, who now is living
in Vienna, a punishment!"

"O tell me that story, Louise dear," the
prince said with a smile.

"Well, then, listen. Your mother had requested me to take this cup to Malmaison, where
the Empress resided. Before going there I had
to inquire after the health of the King of Rome,
whom Josephine loved as if he had been her own
child, but whom she had never yet seen. So I
went to the Tuileries to see the little King of
Rome and his governess, Madame de Montesquieu, who was an intimate friend of mine.
When I entered the room I saw the little king

standing in a corner, with his face turned to the wall. He looked very downcast, and a glance at Madame de Montesquieu told me that he was undergoing some punishment.

"After conversing for some time with Madame de Montesquieu, and taking no notice of the child, I approached him. His face was bathed in tears, and he hid it against a chair that was near him.

"'Sire,' said Madame de Montesquieu to him, 'will you not shake hands with Mademoiselle de Cochelet? She has come here for the sole purpose of seeing you.'

"'I suppose your Majesty does not recognise me?' I added, endeavouring to take his little hand.

"He withdrew it violently, and said in voice almost choked with sobs,—

"'She will not allow me to see papa's soldiers.'

"Madame de Montesquieu now told me that the prince delighted in seeing the guards arrive in the palace-yard, but that in consequence of his being naughty she had denied him this pleasure to-day. When he heard the drums and fifes he

got quite unmanageable, so that she was compelled to have recourse to severe measures.
Thus it happened that he was standing in the
corner. I asked forgiveness for the little king,
and showed him the cup with your portrait, ex-
plaining at the same time the scene it represented.
The King of Rome laughed, and Madame de
Montesquieu let him off his punishment, because
she said his cousin, Louis Napoleon, had been so
good and charitable. That is my story, Louis;
do you like it?"

"I like it very much indeed," the boy
replied, "but I am vexed that the governess
would not let my cousin see his father's soldiers.
How handsome the soldiers of the Emperor must
have been! Mamma, I wish I was an Emperor
too, and could have a great many soldiers."

Hortense, with a sad smile, put her hand on
the boy's head, and answered:

"My son, it is no enviable lot to wear a
crown. It is but too often affixed to our brow
with thorns."

From this day little Napoleon was often seen
gazing in deep thoughtfulness on the portrait of
his great uncle. When he left it, he would run

into the village, call together the boys of the neighbourhood, and go with them to the large garden that surrounded the Duchess's house, to play at " Emperor and soldiers." One day, whilst in the heat of play, he forgot his mother's order that he was not to leave the precincts of the garden, and marched off with his soldiers. When his absence was noticed an old servant was despatched to look out for the boy, and the Duchess herself went with her ladies in search of her son, in spite of the rigour of the season, and the mud that covered the roads.

All at once they saw Louis barefooted and without a coat, running towards them through a muddy field. He looked rather surprised, and seemed to be confused by the sudden meeting. He at once confessed that while he had been playing in the garden a family passed by so poor and miserable that he could not help pitying them. Being without money, he had pulled off his shoes and given them to one of the children, while his coat became the property of another.

The Duchess did not possess the courage to scold her son. She stooped to kiss him. When her ladies began praising the boy for the generosity of his action, she gave them a hint to be silent, and said that her son had done nothing but what was natural and right.

To give to others and make them happy was one of the characteristic qualities of little Napoleon. One day Hortense presented him with three very handsome studs, and the prince gave them the very same day to a friend of his, by whom they had been greatly admired.

When Hortense blamed her son for so doing, and threatened not to make him any more presents, Louis replied:

"But, mamma, do I not enjoy my presents doubly in giving them away? I have first the pleasure of receiving them from you, and then that of pleasing others."

Although this is not the right place for it, still, as we think that no anecdote relating to the youth of Louis Napoleon ought to be passed over, we insert here from Mademoiselle de Cochelet's valuable Memoirs the account of an affair that happened some years previously.

One day Louis Napoleon, then six years of age, had a violent toothache.

"Send for the dentist," he said to Mademoiselle de Cochelet, "and let him pull out this double tooth which causes me such pain, but you must not tell mamma, as it would make her frightened."

"How can you hide it from your mother? her sitting-room is next to your bed-room, she will hear you cry, and will be much more alarmed than if she knew what the matter really was."

"I will not cry, I promise you. Am I not a man, and must have courage?"

Mademoiselle Cochelet promised secrecy, which she did not keep; for the Queen would have been excessively angry had anything been concealed from her that affected her children. Still she pretended to know nothing, in order to please her son.

Bourquet the dentist was summoned and pulled out the double tooth, the child not uttering a single cry. He ran triumphantly to show it to his mother, who was anxiously waiting, and affected surprise, though really more moved than he. No one was ever more courageous than the Queen in supporting the miseries of life with angelic patience, but if her children were affected she was no longer the same woman; she troubled herself about a trifle, and became quite unreasonable.

Two days after the tooth extraction the young Prince had a hemorrhage, and there was no chance of concealing it from his mother, who supposed both her children asleep, and on seeing the attendants enter the room, fancied the danger greater than it really was. It was, however, a painful sight to see the poor pale lad, half fainting, and losing blood from the place whence the tooth had been extracted. In matters of danger for her children the Queen never said a word ; she coolly allowed all the remedies proposed to be tried, but it could be easily perceived what terror she suffered, through her pallor, and the rigidity of her features. After numerous essays, each more useless than the other, the effusion of blood was stopped by laying *amadou* on the jaw. , The poor boy, utterly exhausted, fell asleep in his mother's arms. He was laid in his bed, and the Queen withdrew to her couch, but could not sleep. The next day she said to her attendants :

"I am aware of my weakness, and I was angry with myself about this anxiety, which I thought unreasonable, and, not wishing to yield to it, I tried to think of anything else, in order to fall asleep; but it was in vain—my son's face rose before me pale and bleeding. In a moment my agony became so vivid that I had the notion that it might be a presentiment. I was at first ashamed of yielding to the idea, and then I said to myself, What matter if the idea be a foolish one, I shall pass the night in anxiety; hence I had better re-assure myself by watching my son's peaceful slumbers."

She rose without waking her attendants, took her lamp in her hand, and gently entered her son's room, were all was perfectly silent and calm. The nurse was fast asleep, as was the boy. She walked up cautiously, not wishing to arouse the wearied nurse, and saw her boy, just as her fears had represented him to her, pallid and bleeding.

She raised Louis Napoleon in her arms, but his limbs hung down flaccidly: he did not wake, and the blood streamed from his lips still. By a mechanical movement she placed her finger on the wound which refused to close, and found that a powerful pressure of the finger arrested the flow of blood.

The poor mother could scarce breathe, but she had been successful, and thanked God for having inspired her with the idea of coming to her son. As for him, weakened and wearied, he still slept on; but she saw by his breathing that he was alive. She spent the night thus. Ever at the same spot, not feeling the weariness of her position, without calling up her servants or stirring; and at daybreak the accident that might have been so fatal, was entirely checked.

Happy mother! but still happier son, in having had so devoted a parent. We shall never know what Hortense was for Louis Napoleon; but such anecdotes as these deserve to be treasured, as displaying an amount of maternal affection such as few princes can boast.

CHAPTER XII.

THE REVOLUTION OF 1830.

FATE seemed to be tired at last of persecuting the poor Duchess de St Leu. It granted Hortense at least a few peaceful and comparatively happy years, during which she could rest after a stormy past, and occupy and console herself with the pursuits of art and science.

The Swiss canton of Thurgau had had the courage to brave the displeasure of almost all the European powers. When the Grand-duke of Baden, pressed by France and Germany simultaneously, banished the Duchess de St Leu from his country, it offered her an asylum within its boundaries.

Hortense gratefully accepted the generous offer of the canton of Thurgau, and purchased a small estate on the Swiss side of the Lake of Constance, charmingly situated on the summit of a mountain, that afforded a beautiful view over the picturesque neighbourhood, and the lofty mountains of Switzerland with their shining glaciers. This estate, called Arenenberg, was a charming little possession withal, and Hortense resolved finally to settle there, and had all her furniture brought from Paris.

The house she owned in the capital she sold, and many a scene of by-gone days rose up before her mental eye when she looked at the different articles of furniture which reached her from Paris. They were the chairs and sofas, the carpets and pictures, the mirrors, that had once adorned the *salons* in which she was accustomed to receive emperors and kings. They seemed to her like friends, and she therefore wished to enjoy their company in the solitude of her Swiss villa.

Hortense possessed remarkably good taste.

She knew how to arrange and place everything so as to give it the appearance of symmetry and elegance, her house therefore was exceedingly comfortable and pleasing, and she took a great delight in continually improving it.

When the furnishing of her new home was completed, she went with her son by her side through all the rooms of the villa. As she passed along and beheld all the mementos of past greatness, a feeling of utter wretchedness and solitude overcame her. Where were all the smiling faces that had once been reflected by these mirrors, where the friends who had sat in these *fauteuils?*

Hortense wept bitterly.

And yet there was a certain consolation in being surrounded by the furniture of olden days, they were so many friends reminding her with mute eloquence of a glorious past. Arenenberg was a shrine of remembrance; every chair, every table had its history, a history that was closely connected with Napoleon, with Josephine, and with the proud days of the Empire.

At Arenenberg the ex-Queen therefore at last found a new home. She lived there during the greater part of the year, but when winter came with its snow and storms, when her slightly-built villa began to be too cold, she would go and spend a few months in Rome, whilst her son was attending the artillery-school at Thun.

Thus time passed on. Hortense's life was comparatively peaceful, although now and then interrupted by fresh and very painful events.

In the year 1821 the Emperor died on St Helena. In 1824 she lost her only brother, Eugène, who, after the fall of Napoleon, was known as the Duke of Leuchtenberg.

Hortense had now no one left to love but her two sons, who were growing up into strong and energetic manhood, and of whom she was justly proud.

But they soon became the object of suspicion on the part of France, and most of the European potentates, and were watched by numerous spies.

These sons, with their Napoleonic faces and their dreaded name, were too dangerous a memorial of the Empire to be left out of sight. As long as these princes of the house of Bonaparte were alive, there was no security for the Bourbons.

And yet they lived and thrived—exiles, it is true, and at present condemned to inactivity, but nevertheless young and energetic men, whom events might yet recall to their native country.

There was a time when their triumphant return to France did not at all seem unlikely, when it even appeared as if they would soon be called upon to play a prominent part in history.

It was during the Revolution of 1830, when Europe was shaken to its very foundations. France, who had been forced by the allies to receive back the Bourbons, France rose as one man, pulled down the throne of that detested family, and freed herself from the Jesuits who had found shelter behind it, and given Charles X. the fatal advice to recall the Constitution, abolish the liberty of the press, and reintroduce the *auto-da-fés* and *dragonades* of former times.

France, who in 1815 had been treated like a child, now considered herself of age. She wished to break entirely with the past, and resolved to secure her future unaided and without foreign advice.

The Bourbon lilies had now faded never to revive. A few years of a fanatic and Jesuitical

tyranny had deprived them of their last spark of
vitality.   France threw from her a flower that
was dead, and substituted for it a new and
vigorous plant.

The French throne had once more been
broken to pieces, but remembering the horrors of
the first revolution, the nation wished to avoid a
republic.   France stood in need of a king, and
naturally chose the one who was nearest, and
who for several years past had possessed her
sympathies.   She summoned the Duke of Orleans to the throne, the son of Philippe Egalité.

Louis Philippe, the enthusiastic republican of
1790, who at that time had the three words,
liberté, egalité, fraternité, and the motto, " Vive la
Republique," tattooed on his arm, in order to prove
himself a true republican, and who afterwards
had been an exile and wandered through
Europe, at one time gaining his bread as a
writing-master—Louis Philippe was now King
of France !

The people had dethroned the Bourbons,
they had torn down the white flag from the roof
of the Tuileries, but they knew no better one to
replace it than the tri-colour of the Empire.

Overshadowed by this banner, Louis Philippe ascended the throne. When the people beheld it proudly floating in the air, they were reminded of the glorious days of Imperial France, and, to testify the sympathies they still felt for Napoleon, they asked, not for his son the second Napoleon, but for the ashes of the great Emperor, and the restoration of his statue in the Place Vendôme.

Louis Philippe granted both wishes, and in doing so thought he had done ample justice to the old sympathies of France. He had adopted the colours of the Empire, had promised to let Napoleon watch over Paris from the Vendôme column, and to restore his ashes to France—were not these sufficient proofs of his love for the Emperor?

There was little danger in these measures to conciliate the hearts of the French nation. On Napoleon the dead, honours might freely be bestowed, but it would have been not so safe to treat the living Napoleons in the same manner. Such a course might have endangered the newly-built throne of Philippe, and brought the allies once more to the capital of France.

The hatred the legitimate potentates of

Europe felt for the Napoleon family was not dead. It was for them a question of legitimate principle never to suffer a Bonaparte on the throne of France.

It was for this reason that the great powers expressed through their ambassadors their willingness to recognise the new king, on condition that he would renew the sentence of exile which the Bourbons had passed on the family of Napoleon.

Louis Philippe accepted this condition. The Napoleons, whose only crime it was to be brothers and relatives of the great Emperor, before whom most of the sovereigns of Europe had once bowed, were again banished from their country and deprived of their natural rights.

CHAPTER XIII.

THE REVOLUTION IN ROME.

It was a heavy blow for the Napoleons to be thus once more exiled, a blow that destroyed their dearest hopes, and seemed fatal to their prospect of ever returning to France. They had rejoiced in the glorious July revolution, because they considered it a guarantee of freedom. Most sadly were they disappointed.

Now there was nothing else left them but to continue their previous life. They again turned to science and art, and sought consolation in earnest study.

Towards the end of October, 1830, Hortense as usual left Arenenberg to go with her son to Rome.

But this time she first visited Florence, where her eldest son, Napoleon Louis, had lately married one of his cousins, the second daughter of King Joseph, and was living quietly with his young wife. The heart of the mother was full of apprehension and anxiety. She felt and foresaw that the revolution in France would be a contagious fever, and that Italy before all could not escape infection. Italy was diseased to her very heart, and it was but too probable that in the agony of her pain she would have recourse to desperate remedies and try the blood-letting of a revolution.

Hortense was aware of this, and trembled for her sons.

She justly apprehended that they, who were banished, and without a country, would lend their arms to those who were unhappy, and suffered like them. She dreaded the enthusiasm, the courage, and energy of her sons, for she well knew that if there should be a revolution in Italy this revolution would gladly make use of the name of Napoleon.

Hortense besought her sons to stand aloof from all dangerous enterprises, and not to follow those who might try to lead them astray by the seductive word "liberty," which, in spite of the blood and tears it had already cost mankind, would never cease exercising an intoxicating influence.

Her sons promised to heed her warning, and thus reassured about their immediate future, Hortense, with her youngest son Louis Napoleon, left Florence and went to Rome.

The eternal city, which formerly had always borne an aristocratic and solemn character, assumed quite a singular appearance during this winter. The conversation in the drawing-rooms was no longer confined to art and poetry, or the beauties of the Pantheon and St Peter's; amusement had ceased to be the sole occupation of the city, people spoke about politics, the revolution in France, and were awaiting the signal that was to announce its appearance in Italy.

Even the people of Rome, accustomed as they had been to idleness and inactivity, were beginning to stir, and the police had to hear many a strange and half-forgotten word as they passed the groups that gathered in the streets.

The Papal Government did not dare to arrest the republicans. It well knew that perhaps nothing but a pretext was wanted for the people to rise in open rebellion, and it carefully avoided giving that pretext.

The object of the Roman authorities was to render a revolution impossible, by depriving the republican party of the means and materials necessary for a rising.

Now, the son of Hortense, young Louis Napoleon, was considered likely to give the movement a centre and a name, and it was therefore resolved to send him away.

His very name, the tri-coloured saddle-cloth of his horse as he rode through the streets of Rome, excited the people in whose veins the fever of revolution was already at work. The banishment of Louis Napoleon from Rome seemed to the Papal Government an absolute necessity.

The governor of Rome first addressed himself on the subject to the prince's uncle, the Cardinal Fesch, and asked him to recommend the Duchess de St Leu to remove her son for a few weeks from the capital.

But the Cardinal indignantly refused compliance with this wish. He said that his nephew had done nothing deserving banishment, and that he would never consent to advise his being sent away merely for the sake of his name and his horse's caparisons.

The Commander-in-chief then resolved to adopt more energetic measures. He gave orders that the house of the Duchess should be surrounded with soldiers, and despatched a Papal officer, who presented himself to the Duchess de St Leu and told her that he had been ordered to see her son at once depart from Rome, and accompany him to the frontier of the Pope's territories.

The fear of an approaching popular rising caused the Holy See to forget the respect due to misfortune. The nephew of the great Napoleon was expelled like a criminal.

Hortense rejoiced at her son being sent away, for on leaving Rome he seemed less exposed to the danger of participation in a revolution whose proximity was no longer to be doubted. She therefore gladly consented to Louis Napoleon going to Florence, where his father was living, and where she considered him out of the reach of the political calumny or contagion that threatened him in the Eternal City.

Hence she consented to his departure, which she would have been unable to prevent, even had it been her wish to oppose it. She, a poor, unprotected female, had no one to speak for her, not even the French ambassador would have afforded her assistance. There was nobody to lodge a protest with the government against the brutal and tyrannical treatment of Prince Napoleon except the ambassador of Russia.

The Czar was the only one of the potentates of Europe who felt himself strong enough not to dread the name of Napoleon. He was mindful of the considerations that were owing to the family of a hero and an emperor.

The Emperor of Russia, hence, never refused the Napoleons his protection, and his Envoy was the only one who protested against the arbitrary conduct of the Papal Government.

What had long been apprehended at last took place. Italy rose as France had done; she wished to throw off her yoke like her neighbour, she wanted to be free. It was in Modena that the storm burst. The Duke was compelled to a precipitate flight, and a provisional government, at whose head stood General Menotti, took his place.

But whilst this was going on in Modena, the people of Rome were celebrating the accession of a new Pope to the chair of St Peter, Gregory XVI., who followed the eighth Pius in the vicarship of Christ. The Roman people did not seem to take interest in anything beyond the festivities of the moment and the amusements of the carnival.

But under the smiling mask of popular rejoicing Revolution hid her stern features, and had resolved not to show her face until Shrove Tuesday.

From time immemorial the people had been accustomed to throw sweets and flowers at each other on this day. On the present occasion stones and bullets were to take the place of these harmless missiles, the Roman people meant to doff the fools-cap and appear in their real character, great and imposing, conscious of themselves and their aims.

The authorities, however, had received information of the intention of the conspirators to select the time of the great race on the Corso for a general up-rising, and the festival was prohibited an hour before its usual commencement.

The people disregarded the prohibition, and the revolution, which the government had striven to suppress, began. The thunder of the artillery and the rattling of musketry soon resounded through the streets of Rome. The people everywhere offered the Papal troops an obstinate resistance.

The holy father trembled in the Vatican, and most of the Cardinals lost their heads and retreated step by step as the insurgents advanced. Gregory felt his newly-acquired throne was already trembling beneath his feet, that the Papal tiara was about to fall from his brow; he resolved to invoke foreign aid, and implored Austria to uphold him.

Young Italy, the Italy of hope, enthusiasm, and liberty, turned her eyes towards France. Old Italy had invoked the assistance of old Austria; young Italy hoped for the help of new-born France, where the Liberals had just celebrated a glorious triumph. But France denied her Italian sister, denied her own origin. The revolution had scarce seated itself on a new throne, had scarce clothed itself with the purple of royalty, ere it began to feel apprehensive of its own safety, became reactionary and denied itself.

Rome, like all the rest of Italy, wished to throw off the hateful yoke that had so long disgraced her neck. The entire people became enthusiastic for this idea, and the streets of Rome, in which it had hitherto been customary to see sacred processions and swarms of monks and friars, now resounded with revolutionary songs; the Roman youth carried their heads proudly erect, and displayed courage and confidence.

The strangers and visitors in Rome, alarmed at the sudden change that had come over the city, left it in great numbers, and returned to their respective countries, but Hortense resolved to remain. She knew that she had nothing to fear from the people; all her misfortunes and persecutions had originated with princes.

Hortense had already made up her mind to

remain in Rome, when she received letters from her sons, in which they besought her not to expose herself to the dangers of a revolution, but to leave the capital without delay. At the same time they informed her that they had started simultaneously with the letter, and hoped to meet her on the road.

Hortense was almost beside herself with fear and apprehension when she read this letter. She, who knew and coveted no other earthly blessing than her sons, who incessantly prayed "that *they* might be happy, and that she might be allowed to die before *them*," felt that her sons were in imminent danger of being seized and carried away by the wild waves of revolution.

Had they not left Florence and their father? Were they not on their way to Rome, and therefore on the road to revolution? And could it be doubted for a single moment that this revolution would call them to its assistance, and desire to make use of their celebrated name?

But, perhaps, there was yet time to save them! Their mother's despair, her entreaties, might yet be able to keep them back from the abyss over which they were about to precipitate themselves in the ecstasy of enthusiasm. Hortense felt her courage and energy return whilst thinking thus.

On the very day when she received this alarming letter, she left Rome to hasten to her sons. She hoped to succeed in saving them; in each carriage that came rolling towards her as she travelled, she fancied that she beheld their faces. Alas! she was deceived!

Had they not written that they should come to meet their mother? Where were they?

But, perhaps, they had listened to the representations of their father and remained in Florence, there to await Hortense.

Thus tormented by fears and doubts, Hortense at length reached Florence. She drove up to the house where her son Louis Napoleon had of late resided. Her feet trembled when she left the carriage, she scarcely dared inquire after her son. Nobody had seen him, he was not there!

But, perhaps, he was with his father? Hortense sent a messenger to her husband's hôtel to obtain information concerning her sons. The messenger returned, alone and sorrowful. Her sons had left Florence.

They had both obeyed the revolution which

summoned them.   General Menotti, in the name
of Italy, had asked them to lend their name and
their arms to the cause of freedom and justice;
they had been unable or unwilling to resist the
call.

A servant, who had been left behind by her
younger son, gave the Duchess a letter from
Louis Napoleon, containing his farewell.

"Your love," the prince wrote, "will know
how to appreciate our motives.   We have taken
great duties upon us, and much responsibility,
and have gone too far to return.   The name we
bear binds us to assist all those who are oppressed
and call upon us for help.   Please to tell my
sister-in-law that it was I who persuaded her
husband to accompany me, for Napoleon dislikes
the idea of having hidden from her the slightest
action of his life.

CHAPTER XIV.

THE DEATH OF PRINCE NAPOLEON.

WHAT the Queen so much dreaded had come to pass. Youthful enthusiasm had overruled all other considerations. Hortense's two sons, the two nephews of Napoleon, were the leaders of a revolution.

They organized a system of defence from Foligno to Civita Castellana. The male youth of both country and town rapidly flocked to their banner, and willingly obeyed them as their generals. The insurrectionists, commanded by the princes, were, although but indifferently

armed, and still more indifferently organized, not
deficient in courage.   They were preparing to
march upon Civita Castellana in order to liberate
the state prisoners, who for eight years had been
pining in the dungeons of that town.

Such were the news the messengers brought
back whom Hortense had sent to her sons to
convey letters in which she besought them to
return.   It was too late; they could not, would
not remove their hand from the plough.

Their father was almost in despair about
them.   As he himself was unable to follow them,
for he was confined to his arm-chair by illness
and gout, he implored his wife to do all in her
power to avert from her sons the dangers by
which they were surrounded.   The revolution
was already hopelessly lost, and no unprejudiced
observer could help seeing it.

But the Italian youth would not believe it;
they continued to gather around the standard of
insurrection, they still hailed the revolution with
shouts of joy, and allowed themselves to be
carried away by the bewitching call of liberty,
which rendered them incapable of cool reasoning.

Young men, whose parents tried to prevent

them from joining the patriots, would often leave their houses secretly and in spite of all precautions.

One of the sons of the Princess of Canino, the wife of Lucien Bonaparte, had fled from his father's castle to join the army of the insurgents. He was caught, however, and taken back by force to the parental residence. The family were under great obligations to the Holy See, for the Pope had created the Duchies of Canino and Musignano in favour of Lucien Bonaparte and his eldest son; they therefore resolved to have recourse to the severest measures in order to prevent the young prince fighting against the troops of the holy father.

The Duchess of Canino begged the Grand-duke of Tuscany to lend her a cell in one of the state-prisons of his country. Her request was granted, and the refractory youth was imprisoned in Tuscany until the revolution was over.

Proposals were made to the Duchess of St Leu that she should follow a similar course, but in spite of the anxiety she felt about her sons, in spite of her almost being driven to despair by the obstinacy of the princes, she refused to do so. She would not consent to their being subjected to the humiliation of actual violence. If their own reason, if the entreaties of their mother, should prove unable to bring them back, force must not do it.

Meanwhile the whole family were zealously and incessantly endeavouring to withdraw the two princes from the revolution, and thus prevent their names becoming once more the subject of suspicion to the legitimate princes of Europe.

Cardinal Fesch and King Jerôme besought them in the most affectionate letters to return, and used threats when they found that kindness was unavailing to attain its object.

With the consent of the Princes' father they wrote to the provisional government at Bologna and told General Armandi, the minister of war to the rebellious provinces, that the names of the Princes could only injure the cause of Italy, and that therefore he would do well to recall them. Friend and foe united to damp the zeal and counteract the efforts of the two Princes, and to convince them that they were doing harm to the cause they wished to promote. The foreign powers might perhaps abstain from interfering in the affairs of Italy so long as the revolution in the Peninsula was of a local character, but they would certainly not fail to assume a hostile attitude if they saw the name of Napoleon at the head of a movement which might once more shake the very foundations of their thrones.

The two Princes at last yielded to the strength of public opinion. They resigned their commands, and divested themselves of the rank they had held in the insurgent army.

But although they were no longer allowed to serve the revolution with their name and their heads, they were resolved to continue lending their arm to the cause of Italian liberty. They resigned their commands, but they remained with the army in the capacity of private soldiers and volunteers. When their father and uncles, not yet satisfied, insisted upon their returning to their family, the two princes declared that, if pressed any further, they would go and serve the revolution in Poland.

Hortense had observed a certain sort of neutrality during these proceedings. For she felt they would effect nothing. She knew too thoroughly the character of her sons to admit of a doubt regarding their perseverance in a course they once had chosen, but she was also aware that the revolution had not the slightest chance of success, and that her sons would be lost, if taken with arms in their hand, or at the best compelled to leave the country.

Hortense therefore was actively making preparations to assist them in the hour of danger, arming herself with courage and energy that she might thus be able to make head against the storm, whose approaching menaces already smote her ear.

Whilst all the rest of the family indulged in useless lamentations, whilst her husband deplored the present unhappy state of his sons, Hortense was composed and busy in making preparations for the coming storm.

What she and all unbiassed friends of Italy had long apprehended, took place at last. An Austrian squadron made its appearance in the Adriatic, an Austrian army invaded the insurgent provinces of Italy, recaptured Modena, dispersed the revolutionary army, and deprived young Italy of her dearest hopes.

Now the hour of danger had arrived, now was the time to be up and doing. Hortense was full of courage and energy, she felt herself capable of any sacrifice if called upon to save her sons.

For a long time she had been considering where to go with them.

At first she had intended proceeding to Turkey, and settling in the neighbourhood of Smyrna, but the presence of the Austrian fleet in the Adriatic rendered this plan impracticable. Suddenly a genial idea flashed across her mind, and she saw the way of escape.

"I will carry them off in a manner that will be least anticipated," she said to herself; "I will lead them by a road where nobody will look after us; I will take them through France to England. Threats and humiliations may await us in Paris. What do I care! honour, justice, and humanity cannot yet have altogether vanished from France; no serious injury will be done us. I must save my sons, the road through France is that of salvation, and I shall therefore choose it."

Hortense at once set to work in carrying out her plan. She begged an Englishman who was living in Florence, and to whose family she had once rendered important services, to come and pay her a visit. When he arrived she asked him whether he would undertake to procure her a passport for an English lady and her two sons, who wished to pass through France to England.

The English gentleman knew what she meant, and declared his willingness to assist her and the princes.

On the following day he brought her the desired passport, and Hortense, who well knew that in order to keep a secret it is necessary not to have any confidants, now told her husband and friends that she intended seeking her sons and embarking with them for Corfu.

Her sons were still in Bologna, but within a few days that town must fall into the hands of the Austrians, and all was lost if she could not succeed in reaching it before the enemy. Through an old and tried servant she sent a message to her sons, announcing her arrival, and as soon as night closed in, she set out herself, accompanied by only one of her ladies. She felt herself strong and courageous, for she had to save the only possession that was left her, her sons.

The carriage, drawn by swift horses, soon crossed the Roman frontier, and she now found herself in those districts where the revolution was still victorious, and where people continued to feel hope and confidence.

The inhabitants wore national cockades and tricoloured ribbons, and appeared happy and contented. They would not believe that any immediate danger threatened them.

Everywhere festivities were being celebrated in honour of the revolution and the newly-acquired liberty, and those who spoke of approaching dangers and Austrian bayonets were laughed at and derided as cowards. Instead of making preparations for defence, the insurgents remained idle, and only thought of enjoying the fleeting hour.

The rebel army meanwhile was at Bologna, and had besides occupied the towns of Terni and Soleta, which they had successfully defended against the Papal troops. Everybody was expecting a great, decisive battle, and but few doubted that the Italians would be victorious.

Hortense was far from sharing this universal confidence. At Foligno, where she stopped to await her sons, she spent miserable days of painful suspense. The slightest sound, the rattling of a carriage, would frighten her, for she was expecting every moment to see her sons arrive as fugitives, perhaps wounded or dying even, to tell her that all was lost.

At last she could wait no longer in Foligno. She wished to be nearer her sons, to be able to appreciate the dangers that surrounded them, and if possible share them. Hortense left Foligno to proceed to Ancona.

When she arrived at the first relay house, she saw a gentleman leave his carriage and approach her. He was a stranger to her, and yet she trembled at seeing him. A strange presentiment of evil seized her. The mother's heart felt already the blow that was to prostrate it.

The gentleman proved to be a messenger sent by her sons.

"Prince Napoleon is ill," he said, addressing the Duchess.

Hortense remembered she had been told that

a nervous fever was spreading in the neighbourhood.

"He has the fever!" she exclaimed.

"Yes Madame," the messenger replied, "he
has the fever, and wishes to see you."

"Wishes to see me?—Then he must be very
ill indeed! Coachman, drive as fast as the speed
of the horses will permit. I must see my son."

And on they went with the utmost rapidity.

Hortense was half dead with fear. Pale and
hardly breathing, but without a tear, she reclined
in her carriage. From time to time she was heard
to say in a low voice:

"No!—It is impossible!—I have suffered too
much already—Heaven is just—God will not
take my son from me, he will be spared."

And on they went; village after village flew
past them, they were fast approaching their
journey's end. But the nearer the destination
the more wretched those they met appeared. At
each post-house, where a change of horses became
necessary, the peasantry collected around the
Duchess's carriage and expressed their compassion for the unfortunate mother.

"Napoleon is dead; he is dead," she heard them say at more than one post-station.

Hortense heard it, but would not believe it. These people do not know what they are saying, rumour exaggerates. Her son is not dead, cannot be dead; Napoleon lives, yes, he lives!

And again the people murmured around the carriage:

"Napoleon is dead."

Hortense sate pale and motionless. Her senses were deserting her, her heart almost ceased to beat.

At last, at last she reached Pesaro, and the carriage halted before the hôtel where her sons were awaiting her.

Suddenly a young man, pale, and bathed in tears, rushed through the door-way up to the carriage. Hortense recognised him, and stretched out her arms; it was her son Louis. But when she looked up in his face, when she beheld his pale cheek and his swollen eyes, she knew all.

The people, after all, not her heart, had been in the right—her Napoleon was dead! dead!

And with a heart-rending cry Hortense fainted away.

CHAPTER XV.

THE FLIGHT FROM ITALY.

HORTENSE, however, had no time now to weep over the loss of the son she had so dearly loved. Had not she to save the son who had been left her, a child she loved no less dearly, and in whom all her maternal affection was concentrated? Yes, one son she still possessed! She still had her Louis Napoleon, who now stood by her side, pale and despairing, accusing fate of cruelty for not having allowed him to die with his brother.

Him she must rescue! This thought inspired her with courage and endowed her with strength.

She was told that the authorities of Bologna had already made their submission to the Austrians, that the rebel army was defeated and scattered, and that there were already hostile ships to be seen, which at any moment might disembark troops near Sinigaglia, and thus render all escape impossible.

This news startled Hortense out of her inactive melancholy, and restored her usual energy.

She at once ordered her carriage to be got ready, and started openly for Ancona to make people believe in her flight to Corfu.

Near Ancona, close to the sea-shore, Hortense's nephew possessed a villa, and thither she proceeded.

At times, when the tide was running high, the foam of the Adriatic would plash the windows of the room she occupied, and she could plainly see the harbour and the crowd of fugitives assembled on the shore to escape on board the wretched craft collected in the port.

It was high time for these miserable beings to make their escape, for the Austrians were fast approaching. When the army of invasion crossed the Roman frontier, their commander-in-chief proclaimed an amnesty, from which Prince Louis Napoleon, however, with General Zucchi and the Modenese were excluded. All strangers who had taken part in the insurrection were to be treated with the utmost severity of martial law.

All the young men therefore who had come from Modena, Milan, and other parts of Italy, to assist the Romans in their insurrection, were now compelled to a precipitate flight in order to escape the vengeful Austrians.

Louis Napoleon had to lose no time in effecting his escape, for it might become impossible at any moment. Hortense felt ill and utterly exhausted, but the present was no time to think of herself. She had first to save her son, then she might die—but not sooner.

She was quiet and composed as usual, and busily engaged in preparing her pretended and her real departure.

She intended publicly embarking with her son for Corfu, and secretly escaping through France to England. But the English passport that had been given her mentioned two sons, and

Hortense had but one left. She was obliged to look out for some one who might fill the vacant place.

A fitting person was found in the young Marquis de Zappi, who, being even more guilty in the eyes of the Austrians than the majority of his companions, gladly accepted Hortense's offer, and promised not to interfere in any way with her plans, but to obey her as a son.

After this was settled, the Duchess provided the two young men with everything that was necessary to disguise them as footmen, and had her carriage got in readiness.

While this was being done quite secretly, she was openly making preparations for a voyage to Corfu. She sent her passport to the authorities, begging them to attach the customary signature, and had her boxes packed.

Louis witnessed all these preparations with cold and mute indifference; he went about pale and downcast, and although no complaint ever passed his lips, it soon became evident that he was ill. Hortense sent immediately for a physician, who, after having looked at the Prince, pronounced him to be suffering from a fever that might become dangerous if not carefully attended to.

Louis was obliged to go to bed, and it became necessary that the departure should be postponed for a day. Hortense passed a sleepless, melancholy night by the bedside of her feverish son.

At last the morning dawned on which she hoped to effect their escape. The friendly light of day was gradually dispersing the lingering shadows, when Hortense suddenly perceived, to her utter terror, that the face of her son was thickly swollen, and covered all over with red spots.

Louis Napoleon had the scarlet fever.

For a moment Hortense felt as if struck by a flash of lightning, but only for a moment. Then she felt an energy animate her frame which she had never known before. She at once sent for the physician, and, confiding in his humanity, made him the sharer of her secret.

She had not been mistaken in him.

What was to be done must be done quickly, if not, all would be lost.

Hortense took everything into consideration,

and weighed all chances with the greatest coolness and care. In the first place she sent a trustworthy servant to the magistrate to beg him to sign her son's passport, as he intended to embark that very day for Corfu, and then she secured a berth in the only vessel that was bound for that island. Having done this, she instructed the man to tell the inhabitants of the approaching departure of the Prince, and spread the rumour that she herself had suddenly been taken ill, and was therefore unable to accompany her son.

The physician confirmed this rumour, and told half Ancona of the dangerous illness of the Duchess de St Leu.

After this, Hortense ordered the bed in which her son was lying to be taken into a small room adjoining her chamber, and, kneeling down by its side, prayed God that her only son might be spared.

On the evening of the day the vessel destined for Corfu left the harbour of Ancona. Nobody doubted that Prince Napoleon was on board, and many sincerely pitied the Duchess, who, ill with anxiety and grief, had not been able to accompany her son.

Hortense meanwhile was sitting at the bed-side of her feverish child.

She knew that she too was ill, but she felt no weakness. The great and continual excitement kept her up and endowed her with strength and ingenuity. Two dangers were now threatening her son; an illness which through the slightest neglect might become fatal, and the Austrians, who had especially excluded him from their amnesty. She protected him against both these dangers.

Two days had scarcely passed away, the last two vessels laden with fugitives had just left the harbour of Ancona, when the vanguard of the enemy entered the town.

The commander of these troops, who at the same time was the quarter-master of the army that followed, selected the palace of the Prince of Canino, where Hortense was, as the residence of the commander-in-chief and his staff. The Duchess had expected this, and already withdrawn and confined herself to a few remote rooms, leaving the principal part of the house to the enemy. The quarter-master insisted however on the whole of the villa being given up for the use of the Austrians, and the steward's wife, to whom Hortense had confided her secret, found herself at last compelled to tell the officer that the person who occupied the rooms in question was no other than the Duchess of St Leu alone, ill, and unhappy.

It so happened that the Austrian captain, who acted as quarter-master to the army, was one of those officers who in 1815 had protected the Queen against the attacks of the infuriated mob which surrounded her carriage whilst passing through Dijon. He again proved a protector to Hortense, and hastened to the commander-in-chief, Baron von Geppert, to acquaint him with the melancholy situation of the Duchess.

The Austrian General, firmly convinced that her son had gone to Corfu, readily consented to Hortense's remaining in possession of the rooms she occupied. After his arrival at the château he asked Hortense's permission to wait upon her; but the Duchess sent back word that she was still confined to her bed, and therefore unable to have the pleasure of seeing the General.

The Austrians now took possession of the whole château, with the exception of Hortense's rooms. The sitting-room of the commander-in-chief was separated by a single door from the chamber in which Louis Napoleon was lying ill. The least noise might betray him. When he coughed they were obliged to cover him with blankets, and he was only allowed to speak in a whisper, for his Austrian neighbours would have been greatly surprised to hear a man's voice in the apartments of the suffering Duchess.

At last, after eight days of continual excitement and anxiety, the physician declared that the prince might safely commence his journey, and the Duchess therefore suddenly recovered. She begged the Baron von Geppert to call on her, as she wished to thank him for the kindness and sympathy he had shown her. When the General came she told him that she was ready to depart, and that it was her intention to go to Leghorn, where she would embark for Malta. In that island she was to meet her son, with whom she would then proceed to England.

As on her way to Leghorn she had to pass through the whole Austrian army, the Duchess begged the General to provide her with a pass-

port signed by himself; but she expressed a
wish that her real rank and name might be kept
secret.

The General, full of compassion for the unfortunate lady who was about to follow her exiled
son, readily granted her request.

On the following morning, the first day of
Easter, Hortense set out on her journey. Before
starting she sent the commander-in-chief a short
farewell letter, in which she informed him that
she intended leaving the château at an early hour,
as it was her wish to hear mass at Loretto.

All necessary preparations were made during
the night. Louis Napoleon had to disguise himself as a footman, and a similar dress was sent to
the young Marquis de Zappi, who had been hidden in the house of one of his friends. In this
costume the two young men were to await the
Duchess's carriage.

At last day dawned, the hour of departure
had arrived.

The postboy's horn sounded, Hortense walked
boldly through the rows of sleeping soldiers who
occupied an ante-room, which had to be passed.

Her son, wearing a livery, and laden with packages, followed her. Nobody but the sentinel saw them depart.

Day was just breaking when they started. In the first carriage sat Hortense with one of her ladies, whilst Louis occupied the seat by the side of the driver; the second vehicle was occupied by the Duchess's maid and the Marquis de Zappi.

When the sun rose above the horizon, gloriously ushering in the solemn day of Easter, they were already far from Ancona. At Loretto Hortense went to the church, and kneeling down with her son, thanked God for their deliverance, beseeching Him at the same time for His further assistance.

For there were still a great many dangers to encounter. The least neglect, an accident, might betray them. They had to pass through several places occupied by Austrian troops; this, however, was not the most dangerous part of their undertaking, for the passport signed by the commander-in-chief was sure to be respected. But might not they be recognised by some friends?

Might not somebody feel astonished at seeing the prince, and unconsciously betray him?

On their way to France they had to pass through the Grand-duchy of Tuscany. It was here that they were most exposed to discovery, for Louis Napoleon was well known in that part of Italy, and might be recognised at any moment. Under these circumstances Hortense had recourse to night-travelling. She despatched a courier with orders, always to keep in advance of the party and prepare the relays. The Duchess's anxiety was great, when on arriving at the post-house at Camoscia, there were no fresh horses to be seen. A delay of several hours took place.

They were hours of great anxiety for Hortense.

She spent them in her carriage, terribly excited, and starting at the slightest noise.

Her son had left his seat on the box and sat down on a stone bench that stood in front of the wretched little inn before which they halted. Greatly exhausted by the fatigues of the last weeks, and but partially recovered from his recent illness, he soon fell into a profound sleep, in spite of the cold night-breeze that fanned his cheek.

Thus they passed the remaining hours of the night. Hortense, the ex-Queen, sitting in her carriage, and Napoleon, the future Emperor of France, sleeping on a stone bench.

CHAPTER XVI.

THE PILGRIMAGE.

HEAVEN took compassion on the poor, trembling Duchess; God heard the prayer of an unhappy mother, and allowed both her and her son to escape unhurt all the dangers that surrounded them on Italian soil.

Near Antibes they crossed the frontier of France without being discovered or even suspected. They were now once more in their own country, the *belle* France for which they had been long sighing in vain. That country had banished them, and a sentence of death threatened

the Napoleons if they dared again to set foot on
French soil, and yet a feeling of delight thrilled
through the hearts of both when they crossed the
frontier. Neither Louis nor Hortense remembered the dangers of their situation; they only
knew and felt that they were in their dear native
country again. The air appeared to them purer
and more balmy than elsewhere, while the sound
of the mother-tongue echoed in their ears like
music, to which it was a delight to listen.

Their first night on French soil was passed at
Cannes. The name of this town gave rise to
many recollections. It was at Cannes that the
Emperor Napoleon landed, when he returned
from Elba to France. He left this town with a
little band, and arrived in Paris with an army.
Everywhere the people received him with enthusiasm, everywhere the troops, sent out against
him, went over to his side. Charles de Labedoyère,
the young and bold partisan of the Emperor, had
been the first to do so. He was despatched from
Grenoble with his regiment to check Napoleon's
advance; but on coming in sight of the Emperor
he placed himself in front of his men and shouted,

" Vive l'Empereur." They all followed his example.

Labedoyère had since paid dearly for his
youthful enthusiasm. When the Bourbons returned for the second time he was shot, like Marshal Ney. They both purchased the triumph of
the hundred days at the price of their lives.

Hortense remembered these names, and the
events connected with them, when she arrived at
one of the hotels of Cannes, and enjoyed her first
hours of rest after a perilous and wearisome
journey. Seated in an arm-chair she spoke to
her son of these glorious days. What a difference between them and now ! What a contrast
between their former greatness and their present
humiliation ! Had they not been forgotten, forgotten even by the nation which had once been
proud of them ? The French people had but
lately risen like a lion that, dashing out of cap-
tivity, had broken to pieces a detested throne,
and driven from the country a dynasty that, till
then, had looked upon France as a domain belonging to them.

All this had been accomplished. The nation
had asserted their sacred rights of self-govern-

ment, had chosen a king after their own wishes; but whom had they called to the throne? Was it the son of Napoleon? Was it the Duke of Reichstadt who was pining away at Vienna, looking back with vain regret to the proud days of his illustrious father?—No. It was the Duke of Orleans to whose hand the sceptre of France was intrusted; and the first thing Louis Philippe did after being invested with the regal office was to renew the sentence of exile which the Bourbons had passed on the Napoleons, and which stigmatized their return to France as a crime deserving of death.

"The nation have acted according to their own free will," Hortense said, with a sad smile, when she saw how her son grew pale, and how the cloud of discontent gathered on his brow. "The nation have acted according to their own free will, my son; honour the will of the nation. To honour Napoleon for the great services he rendered France, the nation raised him to the Imperial throne. The people who give have the right to take away again; the Bourbons, who look upon the country as their property, may consider it a domain stolen from them by the family of Orleans, but the Bonaparte family must always bear in mind that all their greatness originated with the people. They must never neglect listening to the wishes of the nation, and always submit to them."

Louis Napoleon looked on the ground and sighed. He knew there was nothing left to him but submission, although the necessity was a painful one. He must steal into his own native country with a borrowed name; in France, in the land of his wishes and his dreams, he was not allowed to say that he was a Frenchman, and his only protection, his English passport, he owed to a nation that had chained his uncle, a second Prometheus, to a remote rock, and there left him to die. But he was forced to submit, if only for his mother's sake, who, deeply veiled, sat by his side as they passed from place to place.

Hortense's stories of by-gone days increased the attachment Louis had always felt for his native country. To be allowed to remain in France and to serve her, was his dearest wish. He would gladly have entered the ranks of the army, even as a private soldier.

One day he came into his mother's room with

a letter in his hand which he had just written,
and which he begged her to read. It was a petition addressed to Louis Philippe, in which he
begged the King to end his exile and allow him
to enter the army.

Hortense read the letter and shook her head.
She was too proud to allow her son, the great
Napoleon's nephew, to ask a favour of a man
who had professed liberal principles, and yet had
not dared to do justice to the family of the
Emperor, but banished them again from their
country. In his desire to serve France, Louis
Napoleon had forgotten this humiliation.

" My sons," Hortense says in her Memoirs,
"although incessantly persecuted, even by those
courts which owed everything to their uncle, always preserved their attachment to the country
in which they were born. Their eyes were constantly fixed upon France, they occupied themselves with the study of such institutions as they
considered beneficial to her, and calculated to
render her prosperous. They knew that the
people were their only friends, they therefore resigned themselves to their will, and thought it
their most sacred duty to serve them. It was for

this reason that my son wrote to Louis Philippe
it was for this reason he so earnestly wished to be
allowed to enter the French army."

Hortense advised her son not to send the
letter, and, seeing that her counsel caused him
much pain, begged that he would at least postpone his petition until they had arrived in Paris.

Louis Napoleon yielded to his mother's wishes.
Sad and lonely the two travellers continued their
journey through a country where almost every
town reminded them of their former greatness.

At Fontainebleau, Hortense showed her son
the castle that had been witness to the proudest
triumph and the most painful adversity of his
uncle. Deeply veiled, she traversed, on Louis's
arm, those rows of apartments and halls where
once she had reigned as Queen. What a contrast again!

The officers and servants who went with them
over the castle were the same whom Hortense had
formerly known so well, but she did not dare to
make herself known. But she felt that she had not
been altogether forgotten by them; she could see
that plainly in the expression of the chamber-
lain's face when he opened the apartments she

had once inhabited, and could hear it in the tone of his voice as he mentioned her name.

Everything in the castle had remained as it had been formerly. There was the furniture of the apartments the Imperial family had occupied after the treaty of Tilsit, in which they had given many a grand *fête*, and in which potentates and princes had been assembled to do homage to Napoleon, and solicit his alliance. There were also the rooms twice occupied by the Pope, voluntarily once, the second time compulsorily, and the little chamber in which the once powerful and dreaded Emperor had signed the deed of abdication, and laid down the crown which the French nation had placed on his head. The chapel also was as it had been in Napoleon's time, when the baptism of his nephew, Louis Napoleon, took place. Everything, in short, had remained as of old, though the garden which had been laid out by Hortense and her mother had grown considerably, and in its trees the wind sang a melancholy song of the vanity of earthly grandeur, and an exile dreary and long.

At last the two pilgrims arrived before the *barrière* of Paris. Hortense was at this moment

nothing but a Frenchwoman, nothing but a Paris-
ian, who forgot all her sorrows and cares in the
pride of showing her son the beauties of the capital. She ordered the coachman to drive over the
Boulevards as far as the Rue de la Paix, and stop
there, in front of one of the principal hôtels. It was
the same road along which Hortense had driven
sixteen years ago, escorted by an Austrian officer.
Then she had been obliged to leave Paris in the
night. She had been sent away with her two
little boys by the Allies, who dreaded a defenceless
woman and two helpless children. Sixteen years
had passed away since that night; Hortense, returning by the same way she had left, was still
an exile and without a home, and the son, who
was sitting by her side, was not only banished
from his country like herself, but menaced by an
Austrian proscription besides.

Still she was in Paris, was at home again!
Hortense wept tears of joy on beholding once
more all the favourite haunts of her youth, all the
streets and squares that were so familiar to her.

It was a strange accident that the carriage
which conveyed Hortense, the ex-Queen of Holland, should stop before the "Hôtel de Hollande."

The windows of the first floor, of which the Duchess took possession, afforded a fine view over the Boulevards and the Place Vendôme, with its column.

"Tell the column on the Place Vendôme that I am dying because I am not permitted to embrace it," the Duke of Reichstadt had once written in the album of a French nobleman, who, in spite of the numerous spies that surrounded the son of the Emperor, had succeeded in telling him the glorious history of his father and the Empire. The nephew of Napoleon was to enjoy this satisfaction which had been refused to his son.

Louis Napoleon might safely go out. Nobody in Paris knew him, and therefore nobody could betray him. He went down to the Place Vendôme and viewed the column of his uncle, which bore testimony to his greatness.

Hortense did not accompany her son on this errand. It would have been too painful to her to pass through the streets of Paris, hiding her face like a criminal. She wished to inform the French government of her presence in the capital, in order to avoid the humiliation of using a borrowed name.

She possessed the courage of truth and sincerity. She meant to tell the King that she had come to France, not in order to defy his sentence of banishment, or to intrigue against him and steal his crown, but because she saw no other way of saving her son, and because she was obliged to bring him to France in order to reach England.

Revolution, which so strangely changes the fate of nations and of individuals, had brought it about that the court of the new king consisted almost entirely of friends and officers of the Empire, who were well known to the Duchess de St Leu. But in order not to expose these persons to any suspicion, she applied to a gentleman unknown to her, and who was too devoted an Orleanist to be suspected of Imperialist sentiments. Hortense, or rather her companion, Mademoiselle de Massuyer, wrote to Monsieur d'Houdetot, informing him that she had arrived with an English family, and had a message from the Duchess de St Leu for him.

Monsieur d'Houdetot followed the invitation, and came to the hotel to see Mademoiselle de Massuyer. He was greatly astonished and deeply

moved when he found that the "English lady"
was no other than the Duchess de St Leu, whom
he believed on her way to Malta. Hortense's
friends, who were equally ignorant of her bold
stratagem, and who feared that the fatigue of the
voyage would affect her feeble health, had already
taken the necessary steps to obtain permission for
her passing through France, instead of continuing
the voyage by sea.

Hortense told Count d'Houdetot of her recent
misfortunes, and expressed her wish to see the
King, in order to speak to him concerning her
son.

Monsieur d'Houdetot undertook to acquaint
his Majesty with her wishes, and promised to call
again on the next day and tell the Duchess what
success he had met with in his mission. He kept
his word, and through him Hortense learned that
the King had said, " He deplored the audacity of
the Duchess in returning to France, and that he
could not consent to an interview with her." The
aide-de-camp added that as the King had re-
sponsible ministers, he had been unable to conceal
her presence from the head of his cabinet, and
that consequently the prime-minister, Casimir

Perrier, would call on the Duchess in the course of the day.

A few hours afterwards the celebrated minister of Louis Philippe arrived. He looked stern and displeased, as if he had come to pass judgment on the accused Duchess; but Hortense's frankness and womanly dignity seemed to disarm him, and he soon adopted a more gentlemanly and polite demeanour.

"I know full well," Hortense said in the course of the conversation, "that I have violated the law in coming here. I am aware of the risk I ran in doing so. You have the right to arrest me, and it would be but just of you to do so."

Casimir Perrier shook his head, and said:

"Just, no! legal, yes!"

CHAPTER XVII.

LOUIS PHILIPPE AND THE DUCHESS DE ST LEU.

THE conversation between Casimir Perrier and the Duchess seemed to have convinced the minister that the apprehensions of the King and his court had been groundless, and that the step-daughter of Napoleon had not come to France to intrigue against them, and claim the throne for the Duke of Reichstadt or Louis Napoleon; but that her presence was solely to be attributed to maternal love, which had made her choose the way through France as the one best suited to save her son.

This conviction removed all obstacles that stood in the way of an interview between the King and the Duchess, and Louis Philippe therefore sent word to say that he should be happy to see her. Perhaps the King remembered at this moment that it was Hortense (who was then still Queen of Holland), who during the hundred days that witnessed Napoleon's restoration in 1815, had obtained from the Emperor a pension of 200,000 francs for his mother, the Duchess of Orleans, and that she had rendered a similar service to his aunt, the Duchess of Orleans-Bourbon. In the joy of suddenly-regained prosperity, both these ladies had written the Queen the most affectionate and obliging letters.

We say, perhaps Louis Philippe remembered this, and wished to requite Hortense for what she had done to assist his family. Hence, he begged Hortense to come and see him, and on the second day after her arrival in Paris the Duchess was admitted to the Tuileries, which, as the step-daughter of the Emperor, and afterwards as the wife of Napoleon's brother and Queen of Holland, she had once inhabited herself. Now she entered them as an exile and a fugitive, without a name and without a suite, in the hope of obtaining protection from those who had once been protected by her.

Louis Philippe received the Duchess de St Leu with all that gracefulness and civility which was a characteristic quality of the " citizen-king," and has always been a distinguishing feature of his house. But under the mask of hearty sympathy and honest friendship he concealed feelings of selfishness and but half-subdued suspicion. Without prelude he began speaking of what he knew the Duchess would wish most to converse on, her sentence of exile.

" I know," he said, " all the bitterness of banishment, and it is really not my fault that yours is not over yet."

He assured her that this exile of the Napoleon family was continually weighing on his mind, and he even went so far as to excuse himself for it, saying, that, properly speaking, the banishment of the Imperial family was nothing but one out of the several paragraphs of the law calculated to prostrate the Conventionalists, and whose renewal the nation had demanded with impetuosity. Thus it had seemed as if *he* had pronounced the sentence of exile, whilst in reality he

had only renewed a law which had already existed
in the time of Napoleon's consulate.

"But," the King added in a tone of joyous
conviction, "the day is close at hand when there
will be no more exiles! I will have none during
my reign."

Then, as if desirous of reminding the Duchess
that there had been exiles at all times, under the
Republic, as well as the Consulate and the Empire,
he told her of his own banishment, of the humiliating and destitute position in which he had
found himself, and how he had been compelled to
go as an assistant schoolmaster with a paltry
salary.

The Duchess heard him with a smile, and replied that she knew the history of his exile, and
considered it one that was highly creditable to
him.

She then told the King with much frankness
that her son had accompanied her on her journey
to France, and that at the present moment he was
at Paris.

"He has written a letter to your Majesty,"
she added, " to beg you to allow him to enter the
French army. He longs to serve his country."

"Let me have the letter," the king replied, "I will send Monsieur Perrier to fetch it, and if circumstances allow it, I shall be happy to fulfil the wishes of your son. I wish you to understand that in every respect I shall consider it a pleasure to serve you. I am aware that you have a claim for considerable sums, and that the state has hitherto neglected to do you justice. Send your bill to me, Madame, write down everything France owes you, but send it to *me*. I know something about this sort of business, and will be your *chargé d'affaires* in future.

"The Duke of Rovigo," he continued, "has told me that the rest of the Imperial family are in equally bad circumstances. I should like to help them all, and will try to assist the Princess de Montfort (wife of King Jérôme) in particular."

Hortense eagerly listened to what the King said. As she looked in his open, good-natured face and saw his benevolent smile, she felt all her doubts and fears vanish. There was not a shadow of suspicion left in her heart. She fully believed in the sympathy and generosity of the King, and thanked him with fervency for what he had promised to do in her behalf.

"O sire," she said, "all the Imperial family need assistance. You will have to make us forget many an injustice. France owes much to all of us, and it is a task worthy of you to help us to our rights."

This debt of France to the Napoleons was an undeniable fact. The Emperor Napoleon had redeemed all the Crown diamonds, even the celebrated "Regent," which the Directory had pawned; he had restored and re-furnished all the Royal Chateaux, and paid for all this, not from the resources of the state, but from his civil list. He had also endowed the Crown-lands with several hundred millions of francs, the fruits of his conquests. When he abdicated at Fontainebleau he fixed his own fate, and that of his family, through the renewal of the treaty of April 11, 1814.

By this treaty he gave up all his riches, all his private property, and surrendered the Crown diamonds to France on condition that a pension fixed by himself should be paid to him and his family. This treaty was signed by Talleyrand in the name of Louis XVIII., and guaranteed by all the Powers, but it was never carried out; on the contrary, all the property and estates of the

Imperial family were confiscated, and they were not even paid the arrears of pension the Treasury owed, and which the Chamber of Deputies of 1814 recognised as valid, and inscribed as a State Debt.

The King once more declared his willingness to assist the Napoleon family. He who was but too anxious to save millions for himself, could afford to be generous at the cost of the state.

The Duchess believed him, believed in his honesty and his friendship, and was delighted with the King's affability, who even presented her to his wife. The Queen, as well as Madame Adelaide, seemed delighted with the Duchess's visit. Once only in the course of the conversation did Madame Adelaide forget that she was a friend of Hortense. She asked her how long she meant to remain in Paris, and when the Duchess replied that she would probably prolong her stay for three days, she exclaimed, visibly alarmed :

"So long? Three whole days? Are you aware that there are a great many English families here who have seen your son in Italy and may recognise him?"

Fate itself seemed disposed to postpone the

17 *

Duchess's departure. When she returned home from her visit to the Tuileries, she found that her son had been once more attacked by the fever. He was obliged to go to bed immediately, and the physician who was called in declared that he was suffering from an inflammation of the throat.

Hortense had once more to tremble for the life of a son, and this son was the last treasure she possessed, the only thing she had been able to secure from the wreck of her fortunes.

Again she sat by his bed-side, watching over him day and night, and tending him with motherly care. To see her son spared was her only wish, her incessant prayer, everything else was trifling and uninteresting in comparison with that. She never left the sick-room, except when she was obliged (as was daily the case) to receive Casimir Perrier, who came regularly to inquire, in the name of the King, after Napoleon's health, and to urge her to draw up a valuation of what the country owed her. His master, he told her, was anxious to meet all her demands.

But Hortense had but one wish now, the recovery of her child. She, however, expressed to the minister her desire to be allowed to visit in the course of the summer one of the watering-places in the Pyrenees in order to restore her shaken health. The minister promised to obtain the King's consent.

"In this way the Government will gradually grow accustomed to your presence," Perrier said to the Duchess. "As regards yourself personally there will be but little difficulty in re-opening the doors of your country, but with your son it is a different thing. His name will always prove an obstacle to him. If he really wished to enter the army he would, before all, be required to change his name. We are obliged to consult the wishes of the foreign powers. France is divided into so many factions that a Napoleon might easily lead to serious complications. Therefore, your son must change his name if—"

But here the Duchess interrupted him. Her eye glistened, her cheek was coloured with the flash of anger.

"What, my son divest himself of that glorious name of which France is justly proud? Hide and deny it as if it were a disgrace to bear it?"

And forgetting in her excitement the suffering

state of her son, she hastened to Napoleon's bed to inform him in hurried words of the proposal the minister had made them.

The prince, with a violent effort, raised himself in the bed.

"Change my name?" he exclaimed, "who dares to suggest such a thing? Let us forget our wishes, mother, let us return into obscurity. You were right, the time of the Napoleons has passed, or—has not yet arrived!"

CHAPTER XVIII.

DEPARTURE FROM PARIS.

THE excitement of this scene increased Napoleon's illness and caused the fever to return with renewed violence. Hortense was constantly with him, performing all the duties of a careful nurse. With her own hands she laid the ice on his head, and aided in putting on the leeches the physician had prescribed.

The continual anxiety and excitement in which Hortense had now lived for many weeks at last exhausted her strength. She felt that she too would soon be ill if her son did not speedily recover, and followed the physician's advice, who told her that daily exercise alone could prevent her succumbing to the fatigue with which she overtasked her frail constitution.

Every night, in the dusk of evening, she left the sick-room, and, dressed in a plain black dress, with her face deeply veiled, walked through the streets of Paris, accompanied only by the Marquis de Zappi. Nobody knew her, nobody saluted her, none could guess that the dark figure passing silently along the streets was once a Queen, accustomed to traverse these thoroughfares in a glittering carriage and hailed by a crowd.

While thus wandering through the streets, Hortense would freely indulge in reminiscences of former days. She showed the Marquis the palace she had once inhabited, and which was still dear to her as the birth-place of her sons. Smilingly she looked up to the brightly shining windows of her former dwelling, in whose rooms some banker or ennobled grocer was perhaps at this very hour giving a *fête*. She raised her hand, and pointing up to the windows, said:

"I wished to see this house again, that I might reproach myself for having felt unhappy whilst inhabiting it. I then complained of my lot, complained in the midst of splendour and affluence—oh, I did not dream then of the greatness of the misfortune that was to overtake me one day."

She turned away, and walked on to look at the houses of several old friends of whom she knew that they had remained faithful to her. She did not dare to call on them, but still there was a great satisfaction in the thought of being near them.

And having thus consoled herself, Hortense continued her walk through the streets of Paris, unknown by the people, perhaps even forgotten by them! But no! not forgotten! Is not that her portrait in the shop-window by the side of that of the Emperor?

She stopped, and in deep emotion gazed at the pictures. A noisy, tumultuous crowd thronged around her as usual; they took no notice of that veiled female standing at the shop-window with a tear in her eye.

"So they do remember us after all!" she whispered. "Those who possess crowns are not to be envied, a person is far happier in the consciousness of a people's love, and the love for us is not quite extinct yet."

The seeming indifference with which France had heard the sentence of exile passed on the Napoleons, had deeply wounded Hortense's heart. She had often wished that she might meet with one more token of affection on the part of the French nation, and thought that she would then return into exile with a lighter heart. Her wish had been granted, for these portraits proved that the Emperor's family were not quite forgotten.

Hortense entered the shop to buy the pictures. When the man that kept it told her that there was a great demand for them, she was hardly able to repress her tears.

She took the portraits and returned home with them, thus to give her son the tokens of French affection.

Whilst the heart of the Duchess was thus divided between the recollections of the past and the cares and sorrows of the present, and she had already been for twelve days in the capital, silent and unknown, the newspapers were extolling the heroism of the Duchess, who had succeeded in rescuing her son, and had already embarked with Louis Napoleon at Malta, for England.

Even in the ministerial council of the King they occupied themselves with this voyage, and considered it necessary to inform Louis Philippe of the fact. Marshal Sebastiani told him that he knew from good authority that the Duchess and her son had arrived at Corfu. He spoke with much warmth of the fatiguing voyage Hortense had before her, and asked whether she would not be allowed to travel through France.

The King looked almost displeased, and replied dryly,—

" Let her continue her voyage."

Casimir Perrier bent his head over the paper that was before him, and a close observer might have perceived a smile on his face; Monsieur Barthe, however, one of the ministers, improved the occasion by showing off his eloquence in proving that a law existed which prohibited the Duchess's presence in France, and that a law was too sacred a thing ever to be slighted.

Hortense's presence in Paris, however secret

it was kept, began nevertheless to become more and more displeasing to the King and his prime minister. The latter had informed her already once through Monsieur d'Houdctot that her departure was becoming absolutely necessary, and nothing but the actual sight of the unhappy Prince, who was just being bled again, had been able to induce him to consent to a prolongation of their stay.

But now the eve of a great and dangerous day, the eve of the 5th of May, the death-day of Napoleon, was at hand. Great excitement prevailed amongst the inhabitants of Paris, and it was with feelings of apprehension that the new Government beheld the dawn of so momentous an anniversary.

Louis Philippe's fears did not appear to be altogether ungrounded. From the earliest dawn of day thousands gathered round the column on the Place Vendôme. Silently they approached the monument to deposit flowers and garlands at its foot or hang them on the eagles with which it is decorated.

Hortense witnessed this scene from the windows of her apartment, and wept tears of joy and emotion. Suddenly a hasty knock was heard at the door, and immediately afterwards Monsieur d'Houdetot, pale and confused, entered the room.

"Duchess," he said hurriedly, "you must depart at once, not another hour will be allowed, I am ordered to tell you, unless it is absolutely necessary on account of your son's illness."

Hortense heard him quietly. She almost pitied a king who had cause to be afraid of a helpless woman and a youth who was confined to his bed. How great must his terror be to make him forget all the laws of hospitality and decorum! What had she done to justify this fear? had she appealed to the nation in her distress and demanded protection and assistance for the nephew of the Emperor? On the contrary, she had hidden herself from the people, and had been so anxious not to create any agitation in France as to confide the secret of her presence to the King himself, that he might help and protect her.

But the Government distrusted her in spite of this high-minded honesty, and her presence, although still a secret to Paris, terrified those who were in power. Hortense could not help pitying them. Not a word of complaint or regret passed her lips. She at once sent for the physician, and telling him that affairs of importance necessitated her speedy departure for London, asked whether the voyage would be dangerous to her son. The physician replied that, although he should have liked his patient to enjoy a few more days of seclusion and repose, he thought that, if proper care were taken, the Prince might leave Paris on the following day.

"I shall leave to-morrow then; please to inform the King of it," Hortense said to d'Houdetot; and whilst this gentleman hastened away to bear his master this welcome piece of news, the Duchess began making preparations for her voyage, on which she set out early on the following morrow.

After four days' travelling they reached Calais. The ship that was to take them over to England was ready to sail. Hortense, an exile

once more, had again to leave her native country,
was again condemned to a life amongst strangers.
Because the nation could not forget the Emperor,
the French king dreaded the Imperial family.
The Bourbons had been openly hostile, had attacked and persecuted them; Louis Philippe, who
owed his crown to the people, felt that it would
be wise to flatter the nation a little and to pre-
tend to share their sympathies. He declared
that he felt the greatest admiration and love
for the Emperor, although he did not hesitate to sanction the banishment of the members
of his family; he ordered the Emperor's monument on the Place Vendôme to be honoured
and decorated, but at the same time he drove
the daughter and the nephew of Napoleon
from the capital, and turned them out of the
country.

Hortense obeyed and went away, but she felt
by the wound in the heart that it was her native
country she left, the country where there was
many a friend she had not seen again, and where
the ashes of her mother and her son were lying.
She had to leave behind her once more the land

of her dearest recollections. Her tears told her
how much she was still attached to it, told her
that, although banished from France, she had
never ceased loving her country, and considered
it still her home.

CHAPTER XIX.

A PILGRIMAGE TO FRANCE.

THE sojourn of the Duchess in England, which country she reached after a stormy passage in safety with her son, was for both a succession of triumphs. All the high aristocracy of London were anxious to receive the Duchess with tokens of love and esteem, everybody seemed desirous to show the step-daughter of Napoleon that the English regretted their unnecessary severity towards the Emperor.

The Duchess of Bedford, Lord and Lady Holland, and Lady Grey, in particular, showed great

friendship and hospitality to Hortense, and were
anxious to introduce her to the most distinguished
families of the country.   But Hortense accepted
none of the numerous invitations she received ; she
seemed to shun publicity, and carefully avoided
mixing in society.   She was afraid lest the French
Government should again suspect her of ambitious
plans, and for that reason place obstacles in the
way of her return to her estate on the Lake of
Constance, to the quiet and lovely Arenenberg,
where she had spent many a year of peaceful
retirement.   It soon became evident that Hortense's apprehensions had not been unfounded.

The arrival of Hortense and Louis Napoleon
created fear and uneasiness amongst many political parties.   They all tried to discover the
motives that had brought the Duchess to London,
for they were convinced that she was secretly occupying herself with some scheme that might
interfere with and be hostile to their own plans.
The Duchess of Berry, who was then living at
Bath, at once hastened to town to watch Hortense.
This bold and enterprising lady was already
making preparations for an expedition to France,
where by means of an insurrection she hoped to

regain the throne her family had lost, and it was therefore but natural that she suspected Hortense of harbouring similar plans. She thought the Duchess de St Leu wished to dethrone Louis Philippe and place her son or the Duke of Reichstadt at the head of the nation.

There were even persons who warned Prince Leopold of Coburg, to whom the great European powers had just offered the crown of Belgium, to be on his guard, as the Duchess had come to England only in order to possess herself, by a *coup de main*, of that kingdom, which she was desirous of giving to her son. The noble-minded Prince scorned to listen to these absurd insinuations. He knew the Duchess from the days of her former greatness, and at once hastened to renew his acquaintance. He showed the poor exiled lady the same friendship and respect he had once felt for the Queen of Holland. They recurred in the course of their conversation to the glorious days of the past, and talked about the hopes and prospects of his own future. Deeply afflicted by the recent death of his beloved wife, Charlotte of England, Prince Leopold wished to seek consolation in earnestly endeavouring to render his new subjects as happy as possible, and was on the point of starting for his kingdom.

When, after a long and hearty conversation, he took leave of the Duchess, he said with a smile,—

"Au revoir!—But you really must promise me not to deprive me of my little Belgium when you happen to pass through it."

"Whilst the French Government as well as the Bourbons, who were exiled like the Napoleons, suspected the Duchess de St Leu of bold, ambitious plans, the Imperialists and Republicans were endeavouring to induce Hortense to side actively with them. In France as well as in England the opinion prevailed that the newly-founded kingdom of Louis Philippe was not possessed of any vitality, because it wanted the support of the nation. The Legitimists, who wished to see a Bourbon on the French throne, fancied that the people were longing for their lawful king, Henry V.; the partisans of the Empire proclaimed the new Government to be on the eve of its fall, and asserted that every Frenchman would be anxious to see Napoleon's son become his sovereign. The Republicans, however, began to distrust the people and the army, and to feel that free institutions would be best promoted by a Napoleon. They therefore began sending agents and emissaries to the Duke of Reichstadt as well as to Louis Napoleon.

The Duke of Reichstadt, to whom the emissaries proposed that he should come to France and appeal to the people, replied:

"I cannot come to France as an adventurer; let the nation call me, and I shall find means to escape from here."

Louis answered the proposals that were made him differently.

"I will belong to France, no matter how. I have proved this by asking permission to serve in her army."

He added, however, that he disliked the idea of using violent measures to carry through the wishes of a nation whose decrees would ever be sacred to him.

Hortense anxiously watched the proceedings of the Imperialists and Republicans to win her son to their side, for she dreaded his being tempted into dangerous enterprises. All she wished was to be allowed again to live in peaceful retirement. She felt exhausted and disappointed after the few steps which she had lately ventured in the public world.

Hortense longed for a return to Arenenberg and the mountains of Switzerland ; she wished to withdraw her son as soon as possible from the theatre of political intrigue. If Louis Philippe would only allow her to pass through France, she might reach the Swiss Canton of Thurgau in safety, where her little estate was situated. There she had become naturalized, and the Emperor's daughter might live in peace under the wing of the Republic.

Accordingly the Duchess addressed herself in a letter to Monsieur d'Houdetot, begging him to procure her a passport from his Government, which might enable her to travel through France under some feigned name.

After much hesitation the passport was promised, on condition, however, that Hortense would not commence her journey until after the first anniversary of Louis Philippe's ascension to the throne. She declared her willingness to accept this condition, and received on the 1st of August a passport, which allowed " Madame d'Arenenberg and her son to pass through France on their way to Switzerland."

At first it was the intention of the Duchess to pass through Paris, in spite of the political excitement that prevailed in the capital, and on purpose to prove by this step how little she was mixed up with the machinations of the discontented; but when she told Louis Napoleon of her intention, he exclaimed:

" If we go to Paris and see the people being shot down in the streets, I shall be unable to restrain myself from siding with them."

Hortense tenderly embraced her son, and replied :

" We will not go to Paris, but we will visit the shrines of our greatness, and pray before them."

On the 7th of August the Duchess de St Leu and her son left England and passed over to Boulogne.

Boulogne was the first of the shrines Hortense intended visiting.   It was the town where she had once been an actress, in one of the grand-

est military demonstrations history is capable of
mentioning; she had been with the Emperor
when he lived in the camp of Boulogne, to prepare himself for a glorious and decisive campaign.
A high column shows the place on which the
camp stood.   This monument had been erected
in the time of Napoleon, but was afterwards made
to bear the name of Louis XVIII.

Accompanied by the Prince, the Duchess de
St Leu visited this column, from the top of which
they enjoyed a wide and extensive prospect of
la belle France, which had once done homage to
their family.   Hortense showed her son the situation of the different encampments, which had
been chosen in the course of the manœuvres;
the spot where the Emperor's tent had stood,
and the place where his throne had been erected,
when he for the first time distributed amongst
his army the crosses of the Legion of Honour.

Louis Napoleon listened with intense interest
and glowing cheeks to all that his mother told
him.   Hortense, sunk in recollections of the past,
had not been aware of the presence of some
other visitors, a gentleman and a lady, who had
listened to her narrative.   They now approached

the Duchess, and thanked her for the interesting sketch she had drawn of one of the most memorable episodes in the history of France. They were a newly-married couple, who had just come from Paris, and told them much about the agitated state of the capital and the hostility of the various political parties.

And as if desirous of giving something in return for Hortense's interesting narrative, they told the Duchess and her son a *bon mot*, which was just then circulating in the *salons* of Paris. It was suggested by some clever politician that the best thing for France would be her transformation into a Republic with three Consuls at its head; the Duke of Reichstadt, the Duke of Orleans, and the Duke of Bordeaux. " But," it was objected, " the first Consul might, perhaps, be tempted to make himself Emperor, and do away with his two colleagues."

Hortense had sufficient courage to reply to this anecdote with a smile; but she lost no time in returning to the town with her son, for the couple might have recognised her and told her the *bon mot* on purpose.

Mother and son returned silently to their

hotel, which was situated close by the sea, and afforded a beautiful view over the surging waves of the Channel.

They went out and sat on the balcony. It was a delightful evening, and the sun, surrounded by purple clouds, was just shedding its last rays over the dark blue surface of the ocean. The air was clear, and the column, near Boulogne, was plainly to be seen.

Hortense had been sitting in silence for some time, now contemplating the sea, now looking at the monument. At last she turned to her son and said with a smile:

"Come, let us indulge in the remembrance of by-gone days. In the face of that proud monument I should like to unroll before your eyes a picture of the past. Do you wish to see it?"

Louis Napoleon nodded affirmatively, without turning his eyes from the Imperial column.

Hortense went into her room, and soon returned with a manuscript bound in red velvet. During the peaceful days at Arenenberg the Prince had often seen her writing in this book; but his mother had always refused giving him any information concerning her Memoirs. Now she volunteered reading to him part of them. She wished to show him, as a counterpart to the sad and hopeless present, a bright and glorious picture of the past, and if possible reconcile him to his position by a spectacle of the instability and vanity of human life. Might not that which had so rapidly passed away return? Might not the heir of Napoleon's great name again behold such days as those of the Empire?

Hortense sat down by the side of her son, and opening the manuscript began reading as follows : —

CHAPTER XX.

" THE Emperor had returned from Italy. The imposing solemnity of the distribution of the crosses of the Legion of Honour had taken place before his departure, and I had been an eye-witness of it. Now the Emperor went to Boulogne to superintend a second distribution of the decoration. He had appointed my husband commander-in-chief of the army of reserve, and sent him a messenger to solicit his presence, and that of myself and son, in the camp of Boulogne. My husband was unwilling to leave St Amand, whose waters he was using at the time, but he wished me to proceed to Boulogne and spend a week in the company of the Emperor.

"Napoleon inhabited a small villa in the neighbourhood of the town, called Pont de Brigue. His sister Caroline and Murat lived in another house close by. I took up my quarters with them, and we went daily to dine with the Emperor. For two years past our troops had been concentrated in sight of England, and everybody expected an attack. The camp of Boulogne was situated on the sea-shore, and almost resembled a town. Each hut had a little garden, in which flowers and vegetables grew, and the soldiers used to keep birds and other pets. In the centre of the camp, on an eminence, stood the tent of the Emperor, and not far from it that of Marshal Berthier. All our vessels of war were drawn up in one line, and only waited for the signal to be ready to sail. In the distance could be seen the coast of England, and her beautiful ships were cruising to and fro, and forming a formidable barrier of defence. At beholding them it was impossible not to feel that the enemy, against whom the French stood

arrayed, was a powerful one, and this feeling created apprehension and doubt. The sea, whose
blue expanse lay spread out so peaceably before
us, might soon be turned into a battle-field where
the *élite* of the two greatest nations would con-
tend with each other. Our troops, who recognised no obstacle, had become impatient at the
prolonged inactivity; full of energy and courage,
they considered the coast on the opposite side of
the Channel already their own. This confidence of
our soldiers, based on their well-known courage,
was conducive to a confident belief in success at
times, but when I looked at the forest of masts on
the other side of the Channel, I could not help
feeling afraid of the issue. Yet there seemed to
be nothing wanting for the departure of the expedition, save a favourable breeze.

"Of all homages a woman can receive, there
are none so flattering and acceptable as those
which bear a military and chivalrous character;
it is impossible to resist them. Nothing could be
imagined grander and more imposing than the
demonstrations and festivities whose queen I was
whilst in the camp at Boulogne; and they produced a lasting impression on me.

"The Emperor gave me his master of the horse, General Defrance, as a guide. As soon as I showed myself in the camp, the troops near whom I passed stood to their arms and saluted me. I had begged forgiveness for a few soldiers who had laid themselves open to punishment, and was everywhere received with the greatest enthusiasm. A splendidly-mounted staff surrounded my carriage, and martial music sounded in my honour wherever I went. On the occasion of one of these rounds through the camp I, for the first time, saw the urn in which the heart of the valiant Latour d'Auvergne was kept. The Emperor, to honour the memory of this dauntless soldier, had ordered his heart to be enshrined in an urn, which was fastened to the bandoleer of the oldest grenadier of the regiment in which Latour had served. Whenever the roll of the regiment was called, the name of Auvergne was read amongst the rest, and the bearer of his heart used to answer, 'Died on the field of honour.'*

* Latour d'Auvergne, a descendant of the celebrated Turenne, was renowned throughout the whole army, on account of his heroic courage, and the bravery he had displayed on repeated occasions; as he persistently declined all the

" One day the staff gave me a *déjeûner* at the camp of Ambleteuse. I wished to proceed thither by water, and the Admiral, in spite of the contrary wind, insisted on taking me there on board his yacht. I saw several English men-of-war, and we passed so near them that they might easily have captured us. I also visited the Dutch squadron commanded by Admiral Versuell. The Hollanders received me with a hurra! They probably little thought at the time that I should once be their Queen.

"At one time the Emperor began the war on a small scale. The English, who felt uneasy at the sight of the powerful concentration of troops round Boulogne, approached nearer and nearer to the French coast, and even fired upon us. The Emperor was in front of his columns when they returned the firing, and thus suddenly found himself between two fires. We had followed Napoleon, and were of course obliged to remain with him. My son did not show the least sign of fear, which seemed to please his uncle very much.

honours and promotion offered, Napoleon appointed him the first grenadier of the army. He fell at the battle of Neuburg, where the Viceroy of Italy erected a monument to him.

The Emperor's staff trembled for his life; the ramrod of an awkward musketeer might here become as dangerous as a bullet.

"I often felt surprised at the contrast our troops offered when drawn up against the enemy and their appearance in barracks. The same men who would glow with impatience to rush to a murderous fight, seemed like children in their huts and little gardens. A bird or a flower would then amuse them.

"Upon the occasion of a *fête* which Marshal Davoust gave me in his tent, some grenadiers entered with the bashfulness of young girls, to sing a few songs they had lately studied. They looked quite embarrassed and timid whilst singing some verses that overflowed with threats against England, and whose chorus, if I remember right, was:

' To cross the straits is not, methinks,
So very difficult a task !'

"From the Emperor's apartments we often looked at the soldiers of the Imperial Guard, who used to assemble on the meadow in front of headquarters. One of them would frequently take a

fiddle and instruct his comrades in dancing whilst
he was playing. Beginners studied the 'jetés'
and 'assemblés' with the greatest attention,
while others, more advanced in the graceful art of
Terpsichore, performed quadrilles. We would
stand behind the drawn blinds and watch them.
The Emperor frequently caught us at it, and
shared our amusement in beholding the innocent
pleasures of his guards.

"Was the invasion of England really contem-
plated? Or was it the Emperor's wish simply to
mislead his enemies by concentrating so powerful
an army at a point where he never intended to
use them? I am unable to answer this question.
I confine myself to the relation of what I actually
saw.

"One day the wife of Marshal Ney invited me
to a *fête* she had arranged at Montreuil, where her
husband commanded. In the morning we went to
see the manœuvres of the troops, in the evening
there was a grand ball. Suddenly intelligence
reached us that the Emperor had just embarked.

"A great number of officers who had been invited to the party rushed back to Boulogne, and I
did the same. I still had General Defrance by

my side, but he was trembling with impatience to be with the Emperor. I myself felt greatly excited at the idea of being present at so momentous an event. I believed I should be able to witness the battle from the tower near the Emperor's tent, and I already fancied I could see our fleet advancing to engage the enemy.

"At last we arrived. I immediately inquired after the Emperor, and was told that he had really ordered the embarkation of his troops, but that he had just returned to his villa.

"I did not see him again until dinner, when he asked Prince Joseph, who was then a colonel, whether he had believed in this sham embarkation, and what effect it had produced amongst the soldiers?

"Joseph replied that, like all others, he had really believed in the departure of the expedition, and that many of the soldiers had sold their watches in expectation of the rich English spoil. The Emperor frequently inquired whether the telegraph did not announce the approach of the French squadron. Napoleon's aide-de-camp, Lauriston, was on board of one of the ships, and the Emperor seemed only waiting for his arrival and a favourable wind to start with the expedition.

"The eight days my husband had allowed me were over, and I took leave of the Emperor. I passed through Calais and Dunkirk, and everywhere I met with troops. It was not without regret that I left the Imperial army, which I believed would within a few days be exposed to the greatest dangers.

"I was daily expecting to hear of the Emperor's passage to England, when suddenly his army passed through St Amand on their way to Germany. They proceeded by forced march towards the Rhine. Austria had unexpectedly declared war. We at once hastened to Paris, once more to see the Emperor before his departure."

CHAPTER XXI.

THE PILGRIM.

On the following day Hortense continued her pilgrimage through the land of her youth and her recollections.

It was a sad journey, this passage through France, and yet one that was not without its charms. The very fact of her travelling on her native soil was a great consolation. For sixteen years she had been an exile and lived in a country whose language she did not understand, and whose inhabitants therefore always remained strangers to her. She was delighted again to understand what people were talking about in the streets and in the fields; she was happy to be once more amongst her own countrymen, and therefore never neglected an opportunity of conversing with them or listening to their talk.

Whenever they had resolved upon staying a day or two at a certain town or village, she would leave her hotel and walk with her son through the streets. At one moment she entered a shop and spoke with the people who came to supply their little wants; at another she stopped a child in the street, caressed it, and inquired after its name. She also conversed frequently with the country people who were working in their fields.

On such occasions she would ask them what they thought of the harvest, and inquire into the nature of their soil. Hortense felt delighted with the sound common sense that generally manifested itself in their answers, and took a maternal pride in showing her son this large and prosperous family, the French nation, to which themselves belonged. At Chantilly, Hortense showed Louis the castle of the Prince of Condé. The forests in its neighbourhood had once belonged to the Duchess, or rather had been part of the property

that had been set aside by the Emperor after the
annexation of Holland to France for her second
son, Louis Napoleon. Hortense had never
before been in this part of France, and could
therefore visit the castle without fear of being
recognised.

Hortense asked the man who showed them
over the place, who had formerly been the proprietor of the forests of Chantilly?

"The Emperor's step-daughter, Queen Hortense," was his reply; "people about here kept
talking a long time of her. It was rumoured
that she went about the country in disguise.
Lately I have heard nothing more about her;
I wonder what has become of her!"

"Perhaps the poor Queen is dead," Hortense
replied, with so sad a smile that her son could
hardly repress a tear.

From Chantilly the two exiles proceeded
to Ermenonville and Morfontaine. Hortense
wished to show her son all the places where, in
the days of her greatness, she had been with the
Emperor and her mother.

Most of these towns looked now as melancholy
as herself. What magnificence had once been

displayed in Ermenonville when the Emperor visited its lord during the hunting season! In the walks of the park that had once been illuminated by thousands of coloured lamps the grass was growing untended, and a half-decayed boat conveyed them to the little poplar-covered island, that was consecrated to the memory of Jean Jacques Rousseau, on whose monument the Duchess and her son inscribed their names.

Morfontaine looked even more melancholy. In 1815 it had been sacked by the allies, and the castle had not yet been repaired. At Morfontaine the treaty of peace with the United States had been signed in the time of the Consulate, and in its castle Hortense had been present at a great banquet given by Joseph Bonaparte, who was then the proprietor of Morfontaine, to his Imperial brother.

St Denis had a peculiar interest for the Duchess, for there was situated the school for the daughters of officers whose patroness she had been. She did not dare show herself, for she well knew that she would not have been forgotten, and her presence was not to be known.

She visited the church, however, and descended with her son into the tombs. Louis XVIII. alone lay in these vaults, restored by the Emperor that they might receive his own dynasty. He who had rebuilt these tombs rested under a willow tree in a lonely remote isle, whilst he who had driven him from France occupied his place in the vaults of St Denis.

In viewing the church Hortense could not help remembering the day when she visited it for the first time with the Emperor, who had come to inspect the works. She had been ill and suffering then, and said what she felt when she told her mother that Queen Hortense would be the first to find a resting-place in the newly-built vaults. Her expectations had not been realized. After many a year she found herself once more in this same church; and was now almost the only one of her family remaining. There was another tomb which Hortense wished to visit; it was that of her mother, Josephine, who lay buried in the church of Ruelle.

A crowd of melancholy recollections rushed upon her mind whilst kneeling on this grave. Of all those whom Josephine had once loved none were left but Hortense and her son, and these two were exiles who came stealthily to weep by her tomb! But the Empress's resting-place was adorned with flowers and garlands, a proof that there were persons near it who still remembered and loved her. Hortense felt greatly consoled at beholding these tokens of affection.

From Ruelle she proceeded to Malmaison. This château especially she wished to show her son. It was from Malmaison the Emperor had finally left France; there Hortense had enjoyed the melancholy privilege of comforting him when he had fallen from the height of his greatness, and of standing by his side when most of his friends and followers had deserted him. But, alas! the Duchess was not to have the satisfaction of showing her son the memorable château that had once been her property. Its present proprietor had given orders not to admit any one who could not show a ticket signed by himself, and of course Hortense did not possess one.

She found herself turned away from the very gates that had formerly been proud to receive her as their mistress.

With tears in her eyes, and leaning on the

arm of her son, she went away and returned to the inn.

They both sat down on a stone-seat in front of the house and looked at the château. At this moment Hortense felt that she had nothing to visit in her native country but graves, that she stood alone and isolated with her recollections of the past.

"It is but natural," she whispered, "it is but natural that those who are allowed to remain at home should forget those who are banished. But the exile himself ceases to live inwardly; for him there is no present and no future, the past is his all! In France everything has moved on, all is changed, but I have remained the same with my feelings and my sympathies. Oh how sad it is to be forgotten, how . . . ."

Suddenly they heard the notes of a pianoforte close by them. The seat which Hortense and her son had chosen was under the windows of the inn-keeper's drawing-room, and these windows were open. The voices of those in the room could plainly be heard.

"Sing us a song, my child," a female voice was heard to say.

"What song shall I sing?" a young girl replied.

"Well, sing that beautiful song which your brother has just brought you from Paris; I mean the song of Delphine Gay, which has been set to music by Monsieur de Beauplan."

"Oh, you mean the song about Queen Hortense, who is represented as a pilgrim coming to Paris? You are right, mother, it is a beautiful song, and I will sing it to you."

The young girl began singing with a clear voice the lines written by Delphine Gay, afterwards Madame de Girardin.

> Soldats, gardiens du sol français,
> Vous qui veillez sur la colline,
> De vos remparts livrez l'accès,
> Laissez passer la pèlerine.
>
> Les accents de sa douce voix
> Que nos échos ont retenues,
> Et ce luth qui chanta Dunois
> Vous annoncent sa venue.
>
> (Refrain.)   Soldats, gardiens du sol français, etc.
>
> Sans peine on la reconnaîtra
> A sa pieuse rêverie,
> Aux larmes qu'elle répandra
> Aux noms de France et de patrie.
>   Soldats, gardiens du sol français, etc.

Son front, couvert d'un voile blanc,
N'a rien gardé de la couronne ;
On ne devine son haut rang
Qa'aux nobles présents qu'elle donne.
    Soldats, gardiens du sol français, etc.

Elle ne vient pas sur ces bords
Réclamer un riche partage,
Des souvenirs sont ses trésors
Et la gloire est son heritage.
    Soldats, gardiens du sol français, etc.

Elle voudrait de quelques fleurs
Parer la tombe maternelle,
Car elle est jalouse des pleurs
Que d'autres y versent pour elle.

Soldats gardiens du sol français,
Vous qui veillez sur la colline,
De vos remparts livrez l'accès
Laissez passer la pélerine.

CHAPTER XXII.

CONCLUSION.

AT last Hortense's melancholy pilgrimage was finished. She returned to Arenenberg amidst the mountains of Switzerland, and lived as formerly in her villa with the beautiful view over the Lake of Constance, with its islands and its picturesque shores.

Honour to the Canton of Thurgau, which offered the dethroned Queen an asylum, when most of the sovereigns of Europe, her own relatives not excepted, persecuted her or drove her from their territories.

In Arenenberg Hortense rested after all the vicissitudes and disappointments of an eventful life. Her heart was crushed by the terrible blow it had received in the death of a dearly beloved son; her mind saddened and bowed by the harshness and cruelty of the world, and beings who in the cowardly fears of their egotism had become untrue to the most sacred and imperishable of all religions, the religion of recollections.

How many who had formerly vowed love and gratitude to her had abandoned her! how many to whom she had been a benefactress had deserted her in the hour of danger!

In the magnanimity and mildness of her heart she forgave them all, and, instead of feeling hatred, pitied them. She had finished with the world!

During the last years of her retirement in Arenenberg, Hortense wrote the sad and affecting narrative of her travels through Italy, France, and England, which she had undertaken in the heroism of her maternal love to save her son. The unpretending and yet talented work is a monument to Hortense's memory, that ranks higher than columns of brass or stone. The latter speak to the eye only; but her book speaks to the heart. It was written after a life of sorrow and disappointment, written by an exile, but it breathes a spirit that is worthy of a noble-minded and patriotic woman.

Its conclusion runs thus:

"The renewal of the sentence of banishment clearly proves that we are still suspected. We have not found a single champion to raise his voice for us, and this increases the bitterness of exile; but I wish from the bottom of my heart that those who have forgotten us may be happy, and that France may be blessed with peace and prosperity.

"The nation, I know, will always cherish our memory, for they can never forget the glorious days of the Empire, its celebrity, its grandeur, and the constant kindnesses bestowed upon France. I feel I have a right to speak thus, this reconciles me to my banishment, and is a consolation I will take with me into the grave."

Hortense lived a few more peaceful, silent years, far from all she loved, far too from the son who was her only blessing, her only hope; little suspecting what a brilliant future Destiny had in reserve for him, and that the Louis Napoleon who had been expelled from France by the Bourbons when a child, by the Orleanists when a young man, would hereafter be enthroned in Paris as an Emperor, while the Bourbons and the Orleanists pined away in a foreign land, in compulsory exile!

In 1837, Hortense, the flower of the Napoleons, expired.

Wearied of the life of misfortune and banishment in which she pined away, she bowed her head, and went home to her great dead, home to Napoleon and Josephine.

THE END.